Charisma Secrets

*Tried & tested techniques to unlock
the magnetic power of teachers -
making them likable, trustworthy,
and unforgettable*

TARANNUM SHEIKH

Verses Kindler Publication.

Website: www.verseskindlerpublication.com

Charisma Secrets

By: Mrs. Tarannum Sheikh

ISBN: 978-93-5605-287-1

NON-FICTION STORIES 1st Edition

Price: $15/INR 300

Disclaimer

Charisma Secrets is written by Mrs. Tarannum Sheikh.

The published work is the original contents of the author and she has done her best to edit and make it plagiarism-free.

The characters may be fictitious or based on real events but they are not meant to hurt anyone's feelings nor portray anything against any caste or system. Any resemblance of names of actual person, place or institute is purely coincidental to carry forward the story.

In case of any plagiarized write-up, the author is solely responsible for it, the publisher would not be responsible for it.

About the Author

Tarannum Sheikh is a passionate educator and a driven entrepreneur. With over a decade of experience in esteemed organizations across the Middle East and India, she founded Active Kids in 2020. What started with just four students has grown to over 500+ students globally by 2024. Under her leadership, Active Kids provides training in communication, creative writing, and conquering stage fright.

She has been a passionate Toastmaster since 2017, actively practicing and sharing her insights with the aspiring community.
Tarannum also hosts an exclusive podcast titled 'GEN Z' where young guests share their unique perspectives on life, school, and the future.

Her mission is to help every child discover and express their inner brilliance, while empowering individuals to unlock the gift of charisma. To learn more, visit www.activekidsonline.com.

Contents

To my husband, Mansoor, who was the first to see the
charisma within me.

Introduction

During a fifth-grade English lesson, a routine day in the classroom, I stumbled upon a word that captivated my curiosity and set the course for my exploration into this realm and that word was '**charisma**.'

At that moment, the term seemed to shimmer with an almost magnetic allure. It was as if the word itself held a promise of something profound and transformative. Intrigued, I delved into understanding what charisma truly entailed. My initial curiosity quickly evolved into a deeper exploration, as I began to connect the concept with various charismatic individuals I had encountered throughout my life.

Three books, in particular, stood out and profoundly influenced my perspective: **Olivia Fox Cabane's *'The Charisma Myth'* and Vanessa Van Edwards' *'Captivate'* and *'Cues.'*** These works provided a treasure trove of insights, blending psychological research with practical advice, and helped me understand how charisma could be harnessed and refined.

While charisma profoundly influenced my journey, the alarming statistic of 44,000 teachers leaving the profession by 2023 deeply unsettled me. This reality hit even closer to home when I, too, resigned from my school teaching job in 2020 to start my own venture.

This transition allowed me to blend two critical realizations—how to harness the power of charisma for teachers. After years of applying these insights within my own venture, working with students, my team, and clients, I became even more convinced of the transformative impact charisma can have on educators and the incredible results they can achieve.

Charisma not only elevated my professional success, but it also brought a newfound psychological balance and fulfillment in my work. That's when

I realized: Why not compile these secrets into a book? A book that could help the entire teaching community reignite their passion for teaching and reflect that joy and confidence in their classrooms.

I understand that teaching can be tough, which is why I've packed this book with practical tips and advice to make practicing these strategies easy and intuitive. You'll learn how the powerful combination of: **Warmth and Competence** can unlock your charisma and elevate you in your role as a teacher, leader, mentor, and beyond.

So kick back on the couch, grab this book during recess, or unwind with it after a long, hard day—you'll soon discover the magic of charisma working in your life. With quizzes, reflection notes, and fun exercises sprinkled throughout, you'll get the chance to reflect on your own experiences and try out strategies that will help you shine.

Forget those emails for now, set aside the grading, and dive into the secrets of charisma—you'll thank yourself later.

Let's dive in!

Chapter 1

Stepping into Charisma Classroom

Charisma is a sparkle in people that money can't buy. It's an invisible energy with visible effects.

-----**Marianne Williamson**

I always wondered how some people just stand out when they walk into a room. There is an ineffable quality about them you can't quite put a finger on but their aura is something you can't overlook. Every aspect of their being draws you closer, be it the way they speak, the way they walk, or sometimes they can be just standing there doing nothing but they still catch your attention. This my friend is nothing but Charisma.

My Early Encounter with Charisma

During your childhood, it is highly likely that you encountered a teacher in your school who was adored by everyone. Personally, I can recall having such a teacher when I was a student. In particular, during my time in 8th Grade, Ms. Sujata, our class and History teacher, held a special place in the hearts of both myself and my classmates. While there were certainly other teachers who possessed great knowledge, such as our Math teacher who was a true Math Genius, not many students felt at ease approaching her.

Ms. Sujata taught in a distinctive way. Every time she gave a lesson, she brought the subject matter to life and connected it to the moral lessons we should learn from the chapter rather than just providing historical details and dates. In addition, she would give us advice and direction regarding our future, the careers we should choose, the morals we should uphold, and a host of other topics that made her an inspiration to all the children in our class.

She has taught me a lot of things, both within and outside of the classroom. I would like to share one particular occurrence with you all, though, as it is deeply ingrained in my memory. Without a doubt, this had a significant effect on my self-esteem and worldview.

Let's go back to the late 1990s, where I found myself in a regular day of class. We were engaged in a timeout activity, where each of us was asked to share our aspirations for life after graduation. It was the typical question of what we wanted to do with the rest of our lives. Ms. Sujata was leading this activity.

Now, I must confess that I had always wanted to be a teacher. From the very beginning, I knew that was my calling. However, as an adolescent, I lacked confidence, and let me tell you, my friend, teaching was not considered a "cool" career choice (and it still isn't). Everyone seemed to aspire to be engineers or doctors, or at least that's what they claimed. So, you can imagine the nerves I felt as an under-confident child, thinking of standing before the entire class to declare my ambition of becoming a teacher. Despite that, I stood in front of the entire class and declared my aspiration that I wanted to be a teacher.

What happened next was like a nightmare for any teenager. The entire class burst into laughter at my revelation. It was a blow to my already fragile self-esteem. Tears welled up in my eyes as I felt foolish and humiliated. All I wanted was to undo what had just occurred. In those few seconds, I contemplated running out of the classroom because if I cried in front of everyone, it would only fuel their laughter at my expense. Why did I even say it? I was certain that Ms. Sujata would also think less of me.

But then, something unexpected happened. I looked up at Ms. Sujata, anticipating a smirk or a chuckle like the rest of the class. However, she came to my rescue like a true warrior. She reprimanded the entire class for laughing at me, rightfully pointing out that without teachers, there would be no doctors, engineers, scientists, or any other profession. Teachers are the pioneers of any career we choose. And as I told you, Ms. Sujata was everyone's favorite, so the class took her words seriously.

At that moment, Ms. Sujata made me feel accepted and valued. It was a significant boost to my self-esteem and confidence, especially for someone as underconfident as I was.

This incident gave a major boost not only to my confidence but my belief to be a teacher. At times, we only need just one person to believe in us and our dreams. Ms. Sujata, if by chance you happen to read this book I want to tell you that I am grateful to you for being that person.

Now to you my readers, this may appear to be a fundamental practice that any educator would engage in. However, it is crucial to acknowledge that executing the fundamentals is a challenge for many of us.

In the present year 2024, it may seem a basic thing for all teachers to adopt such practices. Nevertheless, I implore you to recognize that this occurred during the late 90s, a time when conventional teaching methods prevailed. Ms. Sujata, my History teacher, was truly ahead of her time.
Upon reflection, I have come to realize that what truly set Ms. Sujata apart was her remarkable "charisma." She possessed a captivating presence that

demanded attention, a commanding power that compelled one to listen and follow her instructions, and a genuine warmth that made every student feel comfortable, heard, and acknowledged.

Now, let us delve into the analysis and comprehension of this concept by examining real-life examples of leaders who embody charisma in their every action.

Oprah Winfrey's charisma stems from her ability to connect with people on a deeper level through her honesty, empathy, and storytelling skills. As a media mogul, she revolutionized the talk-show genre with *'The Oprah Winfrey Show,'* which ran for 25 years and became the most-rated daytime talk show in television history.

Winfrey's charisma shines through in her interviews, where she has a unique talent for making guests feel comfortable and understood, allowing them to open up about their experiences and emotions.

Ratan Tata's charisma is his humility, integrity, and visionary leadership. As former chairman of Tata Sons, he oversaw the growth of the Tata Group's global team whose business interests spanned sectors such as steel, automotive, telecommunications, hospitality, etc. Despite tremendous success, Tata remains humble and approachable, earning the respect and admiration of staff, stakeholders, and the public.

Taylor Swift's charisma is based on her authenticity, vulnerability, and relatability. As a singer and songwriter, she has captivated audiences with her heartfelt singing, beautiful compositions, and authentic expressions. Swift's ability to channel her personal experiences into universally moving music has earned her a devoted following and critical acclaim.

ShaRukh Khan's charisma is characterized by his charm, wit, and magnetic presence on screen. As one of the leading actors in Bollywood, he has portrayed a wide range of characters with depth, emotion, and charisma, which has won the cult of millions across the world. Khan's charisma to set the script, on-screen chemistry with his co-stars, and his acting skills are unparalleled, making him a ruler of hearts in Indian cinema.

Barack Obama's charisma is palpable in his eloquence, authenticity, and ability to inspire hope and unity. As the 44th President of the United States, he captivated audiences with his powerful speeches and inclusive leadership style, forging connections across diverse communities.

Did you notice what is common among these personalities? They possess an aura that can be felt even by people who are not in their immediate vicinity, they exude charisma even when you are watching them on screen.

According to a research paper published in 2012 by G. Fond, D. Ducasse, J. Attal, A. Larue, A. Macgregor, M. Brittner, D. Capdevielle, charisma and leadership in psychiatry can be developed through interactions with peers, appearance, and positive reinforcement, enhancing communication and teamwork in clinical practice.

In research, it was also found that there are some qualities that are common to all charismatic leaders. These qualities are self-confidence, high energy levels, and dominance.

There are techniques and actions that you can follow to make your presence and personality charismatic that we will discuss throughout this book.

Yes, with some people it comes easier to them as was the case with Ms. Sujata. On that day, in class, along with the belief and confidence to follow my dream of being a teacher, she made a strong impact on me as a teacher.

The encounter I had on that particular day had a profound impact on my development, transforming me from a self-doubting child with uncertain aspirations into the confident educator I have become today. Despite the passage of almost 15 years, I continue to strive to emulate the remarkable qualities of Ms. Sujata. As a teacher, I firmly believe that if I can inspire the same level of self-belief that Ms. Sujata instilled in me that day, I will achieve success and earn the respect I aspire to.

It is my sincere hope that each and every one of you understands the profound influence that a charismatic individual can have on the lives of others. I understand the thoughts that may be running through your mind at this moment. Yes, I too aspire to embody that charismatic teacher or persona, but how can I attain such a status?

Within the pages of this book, I will lead you through the process of becoming a charismatic individual, offering practical advice that you can readily integrate into your life, ultimately enabling you to evolve into an enhanced version of yourself.

Let us move ahead and reveal the key components of charisma in the next chapter.

Are you ready?

Chapter 2

Unpacking the Secrets of Charisma

Charisma is the art of making people feel better about themselves in your presence.

--- Brian Tracy

How many of you are Bollywood enthusiasts? Then you surely know the reigning star, **Shahrukh Khan.**

My brother, Aasif, a seasoned film editor, has worked with top stars like Shahrukh, Aamir Khan, and Akshay Kumar. Before writing 'Charisma Secrets', my curiosity led me to ask him trivial questions like, "What's Akshay's personality like?" or "Is Aamir really that cute?" However, as I delved deeper into the study of charisma, my questions evolved. I started asking, "Who's the most engaging to work with?" and "Who stands out as your favorite?"

His answer surprised me: *"Shahrukh is my favorite because every time we interact, he makes me feel like the smartest person in the room."* That revelation struck me—charisma isn't just about eloquence or physical appeal; it's about making others feel truly valued.

In addition to this, there are many other interviews where actors, seniors, and juniors, have talked about how Shahrukh listens intently and is completely present in the conversation. Despite being in the position of power he holds, you can feel his warmth in his presence.

In this chapter, we are going to dive deep and decode the concept of charisma together with the three hero components highlighted in the above paragraph- **presence**, **power**, and **warmth**.

I came across this concept of charisma revolving around these three components when I was reading the book, **'The Charisma Myth' by Olivia Fox Cabane,** a renowned French-American author and this made so much sense. I will explain to you my interpretations of these '3 Charisma X-Factors', shedding light on the importance of each one of them for having a charismatic personality.

Presence

Imagine this, you are in a deep conversation with your friend about an episode of your favorite series. You are explaining your favorite moment from the episode and *'ding'*, there is a notification on your friend's cell phone that catches their attention. You continue your side of the conversation but your friend is now glued to the screen of their phone.

Don't you feel annoyed when you are talking to your friend or colleague and instead of you, they are paying their undivided attention to their phone screen, half responding to you while nodding? They are not present with you and isn't that a big turnoff for the conversation?

In today's world of Instagram and TikTok, with everyone's attention span becoming shorter each day, if you are a person who knows to be present during your interactions with people, you have won a big part of the quest for cultivating charisma with your presence.
Being present and giving your undivided attention to the person in front of you makes them feel that they are getting connected with you, that they are

forging a connection with you, and that you have some commonalities. When they feel that you have similarities, your presence will attract them.

Researchers Dr. Ellen Berscheid, an American social psychologist and Dr. Elaine Walster, an academic researcher from the University of Wisconsin-Madison found out that we enjoy our time around people who are similar to us. It gives us a sense of validation that the person we are speaking to understands us and we have a common ground.

Most of us in the middle of a conversation, are absent with the intent to listen and understand. Even if we are not looking at the screens of our phones, we are constantly wandering in our minds to come up with witty and clever responses to what the person is saying.

In fact, the author of '**Captivate**', **Vanessa Van Edwards,** a body language and behaviour expert specializing in science-based people skills had a similar problem. Let's talk about one of the incidents she shared in her book in chapter

She took a **'Vow of Silence'** to become a better listener for one full week. She did it because one of her friends mentioned to her that she was an 'interrupter' in conversations.

She mentioned in her book, *"I am terrified of awkward silences. I fear that moment, when someone finishes a sentence and no one knows what to say next. To prevent these uncomfortable pauses, I got in the habit of interrupting. Worse, I began to prepare my responses while only half listening to the conversation. This is a terrible way to interact–it's disrespectful, inauthentic, and exhausting for all the parties."*

After this self-reflection, she decided to take a 'Vow of silence' for one week. She attended all her business meetings, conferences, and get-togethers with the sole intent of being a better listener. She only communicated with people through her four premade flash cards.

To her surprise, she made better business connections in her silent week than during the fast-paced industry conference she had attended a week before.

According to a 2,250-person study, co-authored by Harvard psychologist Daniel Gilbert, nearly half of the average person's time was spent 'mind wandering'. The key is to be conscious when your mind is wandering and make a habit of going back to listening intently when this happens.

It is evident that as individuals, we have an innate desire for others to lend us their ears. The true power of our presence lies in the moments when we are fully engaged with those around us. Now I know what you are thinking. *"Even when I am trying to be fully present in a conversation without allowing any external distractions, my mind still wanders here and there during the conversation from time to time."* **I understand your concern** - even when we strive to be fully present, our minds may occasionally wander during conversations. Rest assured, this is a common occurrence that happens to everyone.

Being fully present in small intervals from time to time will help you have a considerable impact.

Putting it into Practice

- **Scan the sounds** you hear, notice your breathing patterns, and feel the sensations in your toes. When you practice these techniques, it helps you stay truly present in the moment.

- **Practice meditation and mindfulness,** and listen to the sound of the universe, the birds, and the fan (and everything for that matter). Be aware of your surroundings.
- Don't make everything about **'yourself'** when interacting with someone. Instead, make them feel important and truly heard.
- Be the **star of the conversation** by making the other people with you feel like a star when they are interacting with you.

Power

Having a presence makes people want to talk to you, but having power makes people want to listen to what you say. Think back to your school days. Some teachers could command your attention effortlessly, while others struggled to hold it for even a minute. The difference lay in their projection of power.

Power, in this context, is not about authoritarian control but rather about confidence, competence, and the ability to influence others positively. Confident individuals exude a presence that captivates and commands respect, not through force, but through the strength of their convictions and the clarity of their communication.

In the context of charisma, power refers to the ability of an individual to influence and impact others effectively. It encompasses the capacity to lead, inspire, and achieve goals through various means, including expertise, likability, and formal authority. Power in charisma is multifaceted and can derive from different sources. Expert power arises from deep knowledge and skills in a particular domain, enabling individuals to influence others based on their expertise and credibility.

Referent power comes from **likability, trust, and connection** with others, where individuals inspire loyalty and admiration due to their warmth and ability to relate to others. Informational power stems from access to valuable information and the ability to communicate it effectively, providing insights that guide decisions and actions. Lastly, positional power comes from formal authority within organizational hierarchies, granting individuals the ability to make decisions and direct others.

Effective leaders who possess power in charisma know how to balance it with warmth and competence. Warmth in charisma includes traits like kindness, empathy, and genuineness, which help leaders build trust and rapport with their teams. Competence, on the other hand, involves skills, expertise, and a track record of achieving results, which are essential for gaining respect and credibility. By combining power with warmth and competence, leaders create a compelling presence that motivates and inspires their teams. *(Detailed analysis in chapter 3)*

But how to exude power and make your presence feel powerful?

Being prepared with the points you want to discuss gives you an edge which helps you feel confident. As a result of the domino effect, when you feel confident, the person you are conversing with can sense your confidence and it is more likely that you will be taken seriously. Think about the time when you take an exam, if you have studied diligently, you are less likely to have the jitters that come with the pressure of taking the exam.

There are many ways you may boost and feel confident. Some of us feel confident when we are looking good, and are dressed sharply. Having a fit body and feeling comfortable in our body also gives us confidence a major confidence boost. You need to figure out what works for you. You need to present yourself feeling confident and comfortable about yourself. Try to be authentic and true to yourself in the process. Don't try to fake it because people will catch it.

When you are trying to fake it people will catch that in the way you interact, both with your body language and words. And if you are thinking that you can divert people's attention before they notice it, you are wrong my friend. Do you know why?

Because the human mind can read facial expressions in as little as seventeen milliseconds. No matter how fast you are, you can't deceive people.

Remember your mind should feel what you are trying to project because our body language is a reflection of what we are thinking in our minds.

Are you a fan of cricket? Well, if you were born in India, whether you are a fan or not, I am sure you have been forced to watch the game with your father and brother.

Have you noticed the body language of a fielder when he drops a catch?

When a player drops a catch in the field, their body language can convey a mix of emotions and reactions. Initially, there might be a visible moment of shock or disbelief, often accompanied by a sudden tensing of the muscles as they realize what just happened. This could manifest as a sudden freeze or a jerky movement.

Following this initial reaction, the player might display signs of frustration or disappointment. This could include slumping of the shoulders, hanging off the head, or even kicking at the ground in frustration. Their facial expression might range from a grimace to a look of frustration or embarrassment. You are able to see and comprehend all of their emotions in their mind by just watching how their body is responding to the situation.

The same is true for a vice-versa situation. When a player successfully catches the ball in cricket, their body language typically reflects a mix of elation and concentration. Initially, there's a quick burst of excitement, often manifested through a wide smile, raised arms, or a triumphant fist pump. The player might leap in the air or take a few quick steps in celebration. This immediate reaction is followed by a moment of focus and composure, as they quickly regain their stance and assess the situation on the field. Despite the adrenaline rush, their body language remains controlled and poised, conveying a sense of readiness for the next play. Overall, the fielder's behavior showcases a blend of joy, confidence, and readiness to continue contributing to the team's success.

That is the importance of how you feel in your mind in projecting your power in a situation because no matter what you say when your nonverbal cues contradict your speech, you will lose the game of power. We will delve into non-verbal cues in detail in that chapter to help you master the art of sending the right cues through your body.

Putting it into Practice

- **Prep yourself** before any important meeting or presentation by jotting down the important points to be covered on a piece of paper or on your laptop. This helps you feel confident.
- **Identify** the things that help you feel more confident and do those things to boost your confidence. It can be dressing sharply, hitting the gym for a better body, or applying some makeup before your important meeting or lecture.
- Be **conscious** and **mindful** of the thoughts you are having because your face is a reflection of the thoughts in your mind.

- As soon as a **negative thought** comes up, train your mind to leave it to the greater force of the universe. It alleviates the weight from your mind and body to feel relaxed and comfortable

- Be **authentic** and increase your projection of power by playing to your strengths.

Warmth

Let's now assess your attentiveness to the first chapter. As you may recall, we discussed our history teacher, Ms. Sujata, who was adored by everyone in school. Surprisingly, even though our Math teacher was exceptionally talented, Ms. Sujata was the preferred choice. Upon further reflection, I realized that while our Math teacher possessed brilliance and a commanding presence, she lacked the essential element of warmth. This absence of warmth prevented us, as students, from forming a deep connection with her. On the other hand, it was Ms. Sujata's warmth and her ability to empathize with students, in addition to her power and presence, that made her an exceptional teacher.

Warmth is the glue that binds charisma together, adding depth and resonance to one's presence and power.

Understanding Warmth in Charisma

Warmth is a fundamental component of charisma that enhances an individual's presence and impact. It involves creating a positive emotional connection with others through genuine care, empathy, and respect. While power commands attention and authority, warmth is what builds trust, rapport, and lasting relationships.

Warmth has a profound psychological impact on human interactions. It fosters a sense of safety and comfort, making people feel valued and appreciated.

Research in social psychology suggests that warmth is a critical factor in forming positive impressions and building long-term relationships. When people perceive someone as warm, they are more likely to trust them, cooperate with them, and feel motivated to engage with them.

Warmth elicits positive emotional responses from others. Research in psychology has shown that positive emotions are contagious and can significantly impact social interactions. When teachers or leaders display warmth, they create an atmosphere where students or followers feel valued, appreciated, and motivated to engage.

For instance, studies have shown that leaders who exhibit warmth are rated higher in terms of their effectiveness and the willingness of their team members to follow them. This is because warmth signals approachability, understanding, and a genuine concern for others' well-being. In educational settings, teachers who demonstrate warmth are more successful in creating supportive learning environments where students feel encouraged to participate and learn.

If a person has only power and no warmth, you may feel like avoiding that person at times, because that person's presence will make you feel inferior. We are wired to avoid anything that makes us feel inferior. But when your presence has the right balance of warmth and power, your charisma will be felt by people in your vicinity.

And you know what the best part is you don't have to go overboard to learn and practice warmth. Warmth is reflected in small gestures, such as a sincere smile, a listening ear, or a comforting touch. It's about making others feel appreciated and respected, regardless of their status or background.

Charismatic leaders who exude warmth are approachable and relatable, making it easy for others to connect with them on a personal level.

Ultimately, warmth is the heart of charisma, amplifying the impact of one's presence and power. It's a quality that extends beyond verbal and physical expressions, leaving a lasting impression on those around us.

Putting it into Practice

- Offer **genuine compliments** and appreciation to people around you. Don't be fake, be genuine with your praises and appreciation.
- Practice **small acts of kindness** like holding the door open, offering to help, or remembering someone's birthday can show warmth and consideration.
- **Remember the names** of the people and use their names in your interactions. Hearing one's own name is the favorite sound to the ear of human beings. It fosters a sense of connection and rapport.
- **Practice active listening**. Show empathy by nodding and paraphrasing to demonstrate understanding.

When you have the right balance of presence, power, and warmth in your interactions, your conversations and encounters with people become charismatic. Incorporating these behaviors may take some time. You know the best way to do it- practice.

Now that you have understood the importance of presence, power, and warmth, you are ready to learn how they pave the way for our exploration of charisma cues in the next chapter.

<h1 style="text-align:center">Key Takeaways</h1>

- **Be fully present:** Practice active listening and mindfulness to fully engage in conversations, demonstrating that you value the person you're interacting with.

- **Cultivate confidence and competence:** Prepare thoroughly and speak with conviction to convey power and authority, making others more likely to listen and respect your opinions.

- **Show warmth and empathy:** Use small gestures of kindness and empathy, such as remembering names and offering genuine compliments, to build trust and make meaningful connections.

- **Balance Presence, Power, and Warmth:** A combination of these three factors is essential for charisma. Strive for a balance where each aspect complements the others.

- **Practice makes perfect:** Developing charisma takes practice. Incorporate these behaviors into your daily interactions to enhance your charisma over time.

Chapter 3

The Charisma Formula

Charisma is the perfect blend of warmth and confidence.
----**Vanessa Van Edwards**

Charisma, often seen as an enigmatic and rare quality, is increasingly understood through the lens of modern research and theory. Two prominent perspectives on charisma come from Olivia Fox Cabane and Vanessa Van Edwards, who highlight remarkably similar components despite using slightly different terminology. Olivia Fox Cabane's theory of charisma identifies three key elements: **presence, power, and warmth.** Meanwhile, Vanessa Van Edwards simplifies charisma into two core traits: **warmth and competence.** Understanding the interplay between these elements provides a comprehensive framework for developing and harnessing charisma in personal and professional settings.

Olivia Fox Cabane's model emphasizes the importance of being fully present in interactions, projecting power through confidence and authority, and exuding warmth to connect with others on a personal level. Presence is about giving your full attention to the moment, making others feel valued and understood. Power, in this context, is the ability to influence and command respect, while warmth relates to your approachability and empathy. Together, these elements create a magnetic personality that draws people in and inspires trust and admiration.

Vanessa Van Edwards, on the other hand, focuses on warmth and competence. Warmth, as defined by both theories, encompasses kindness, friendliness, and trustworthiness, forming the foundation of likability. Competence aligns closely with power in Cabane's model, signifying expertise, skill, and reliability. When combined, warmth and competence form a powerful duo that makes a person both likable and respectable. Vanessa's research indicates that the most charismatic individuals strike a balance between these traits, leading to higher social influence and better personal and professional relationships.

During my research for writing this book, I came across Vanessa Van Edward's book called "Cues". In her book, she has simplified the concept of charisma. She mentions in her book, "*In a groundbreaking study from Princeton University, researchers found that highly charismatic, likable, compelling people demonstrate a special blend of two specific traits: warmth and competence.*"

The theories of charisma by Olivia Fox Cabane and Vanessa Van Edwards are interrelated through their emphasis on similar foundational elements—presence, power, and warmth (Cabane) align closely with warmth and competence (Van Edwards). Together, these models provide a comprehensive framework for understanding and cultivating charisma, highlighting the importance of balancing emotional connection with professional competence.

What is competence and warmth?

Competence is the ability to do something well or effectively. It shows your expertise. It refers to the combination of a person's knowledge, skills, experience, and training, along with their ability to apply those skills to perform a task diligently whereas **warmth** is a combination of kindness, friendliness, helpfulness, generosity, and trustworthiness. It highly contributes to your likability as a person.

Warmth and competence when used wisely with a balance in our interactions, they hit a sweet spot for charisma.

My First Venture with Competence and Warmth

On my first day teaching Grades 1 to 5 at a new school, I attended a team meeting where the Head of Department (HOD) introduced me to the other teachers. To ease my start, the HOD assigned me a simple task: create a presentation about the school, my teaching approach, and areas for improvement by Wednesday. I could seek help from experienced colleagues.

I observed three colleagues: the first, praised for her skills, was reserved; the second was very friendly but not taken seriously by others, making me question her competence; the third was warm, welcoming, and offered insightful comments. I chose to seek help from the third teacher, who seemed both knowledgeable and approachable. This experience showed how our judgments are often based on the cues people give during interactions.

What are Cues?

As per Vanessa Van Edwards, "Cues are the powerful verbal, nonverbal and vocal signals humans send to each other."

Our brain is constantly analyzing the cues we get from our surroundings. Based on the cues our brain receives, it categorizes the people in a particular box in our memory.

And that's how we remember a person's personality.

Studies by Susan Fiske and Amy Cuddy have shown that we judge people primarily by two criteria: their warmth and their competence.

We analyze the cues we are getting and decide which one is the dominant personality trait.

Many people believe that you should be highly competent in your professional life and highly warm in your personal life. While it is true that displaying competence in your professional life will work but if you don't blend it with the required warmth, you may come across as a person who thinks too highly of themselves, arrogant, unapproachable, or "difficult to work with".

Yes, showing your competence in professional life is a must because you want to be taken seriously by your boss and the colleagues you are working with. If you want to get ahead in your career, competence is a must. But being only competent may not always work in your favor. Warmth is a lubricant for competence.

Especially if you are a teacher, along with being competent in your subjects, you should have warmth so that students can connect with you. Only when they are able to connect with you, will they develop a keen interest in the subject and lectures you are delivering. Only when you have a **balance of competence and warmth,** you will be able to deal with students and their parents effectively.

In any job, including teaching, it's crucial to balance warmth with competence. If you're warm but lack competence, you risk not being taken seriously by students, parents, and colleagues. This can lead to being seen as a pushover. While it may seem unfair, we all judge and are judged based on cues we send. Think about how you describe people you meet: words like "sweet" and "nice" indicate warmth, while "confident" and "smart" indicate competence. The most memorable people are those who display both qualities.

Now you may be either high on sending warmth cues but low on sending competent cues or you may be high on sending competence cues and low on warmth cues. Let's try to understand what happens if one is dominant over the other.

Higher in Competence

When an individual is high in competence but low in warmth, they are often perceived as highly capable and knowledgeable, but also as unapproachable, intimidating, or untrustworthy. This combination can lead to mixed reactions from others, such as respect for their skills but reluctance to engage with them on a personal level.

Example: A High-Performing Manager with Low Warmth

Consider a high-performing manager, Sarah, in a corporate setting. Sarah is exceptionally competent in her role. She consistently meets her targets, delivers high-quality work, and has a deep understanding of the industry. Her analytical skills and strategic thinking are top-notch, making her an asset to the company in terms of achieving business goals.

However, Sarah's interpersonal skills leave much to be desired. She rarely smiles, her body language is often closed off, and she doesn't engage in small talk with her colleagues. Sarah's communication style is direct and to the point, often coming across as blunt or harsh. She doesn't offer praise or show appreciation for her team's efforts, focusing instead on what needs to be done next or pointing out mistakes.

Impact on Team Dynamics

- Respect and Fear: Sarah's team respects her for her knowledge and ability to solve problems efficiently. They acknowledge her as an expert in her field and often seek her advice on technical matters. However, this respect is tinged with fear. Team members are apprehensive about approaching her with questions or concerns, worried about receiving a curt response or being made to feel inadequate.
- Low Morale: The lack of warmth from Sarah leads to low morale within the team. With positive reinforcement and a sense of personal connection, employees feel more valued and motivated. This can result in higher turnover rates, as employees seek a more supportive and engaging work environment elsewhere.
- Ineffective Collaboration: Effective collaboration requires trust and open communication, which are hampered by Sarah's low warmth. Team members may be reluctant to share ideas or feedback, leading to missed opportunities for innovation and improvement. The atmosphere becomes one where individuals work in silos rather than as a cohesive unit.

Long-Term Consequences

In the long run, Sarah's high competence may not be enough to sustain her success if she cannot build positive relationships with her team and colleagues. While her technical skills and knowledge are invaluable, her lack of warmth can lead to a toxic work environment, decreased productivity, and ultimately, a decline in her effectiveness as a leader.

Being high in competence but low in warmth creates a challenging dynamic. The individual may achieve short-term success due to their skills and expertise, but they risk long-term failure if they cannot foster trust and positive relationships. Balancing competence with warmth is crucial for sustainable success and effective leadership.

Putting it into Practice

- **Smile sincerely:** Start your interactions with a warm and genuine smile. A smile can instantly make others feel comfortable and welcomed. Remember, a smile is contagious! (Think about it. Even if you are having a bad day when you see a genuine smile directed towards you, it uplifts your mood a little, right?)
- **Use open body language:** Keep your body language open and inviting. Avoid crossing your arms or standing with a rigid posture. Instead, maintain relaxed and open gestures to signal approachability.
- **Show interest:** Demonstrate a genuine interest in others by actively listening to what they say. Ask open-ended questions and show empathy by acknowledging their feelings and experiences.
- **Offer genuine compliments:** Take the time to compliment others sincerely. Whether it's praising their work, style, or personality, genuine compliments can make a person feel valued and appreciated.
- **Practice active listening:** Focus on listening intently to what others are saying without interrupting or judgment. Reflect on what they've shared to show that you understand and care about their perspective.
- **Remember names:** Make an effort to remember people's names and use them in conversation. Using someone's name can create a sense of connection and personalization.
- **Share personal stories:** Be willing to share anecdotes or personal stories that others can relate to. Sharing a bit of yourself can help foster a deeper connection and mutual understanding.
- **Offer support:** Be there to offer support and assistance when needed. Whether it's lending a listening ear, offering a helping hand, or providing words of encouragement, small gestures of support can go a long way.

- **Express gratitude:** Express gratitude for the presence and contributions of others. A simple "thank you" can convey appreciation and warmth.
- **Spread positivity:** Maintain a positive and uplifting attitude in your interactions. Offer words of encouragement, share laughter, and focus on creating a positive atmosphere wherever you go.

Higher in Warmth

When an individual is high in warmth but low in competence, they are often perceived as friendly, approachable, and well-liked, but they may struggle to be taken seriously in professional settings due to a lack of skills or expertise. This combination can lead to an environment where people enjoy their company but question their effectiveness in fulfilling their responsibilities.

Example: A Friendly but Inexperienced Team Leader

Consider John, a team leader in a marketing firm. John is exceptionally warm and approachable. He always greets his colleagues with a smile, remembers personal details about their lives, and makes a point of offering encouragement and praise. His positive attitude and friendly demeanor make him a favorite among his peers, and he is well-liked by everyone in the office.

Impact on Team Dynamics

- High Morale but Low Productivity: John's warmth creates a pleasant and supportive work environment. Team members feel valued and are comfortable approaching him with their problems or ideas. However, John's lack of competence becomes evident when it comes to making strategic decisions, managing projects, or solving complex problems.

He often struggles to provide clear direction or make informed decisions, leading to confusion and inefficiency.

- Dependence on Others: Due to his low competence, John frequently relies on more knowledgeable team members to fill in the gaps. While this can foster collaboration, it can also lead to frustration among those who feel they are carrying an unfair share of the workload. Over time, this reliance can erode respect for John's leadership, even if he remains personally liked.

- Missed Opportunities: John's inability to effectively manage projects or leverage opportunities can result in missed deadlines and suboptimal performance. Despite the positive atmosphere, the team's overall productivity and success suffer because they lack the guidance and expertise needed to excel.

Long-Term Consequences

In the long run, John's high warmth but low competence may lead to dissatisfaction and disengagement among team members who are eager to achieve more and grow professionally. The team's performance may stagnate, and high-performing employees might leave the company in search of more competent leadership. Additionally, John's career progression could be hindered as his lack of competence becomes a barrier to taking on greater responsibilities or higher roles within the organization.

While being high in warmth creates a supportive and positive environment, it is not sufficient for effective leadership or professional success if not paired with competence. Individuals like John can maintain personal popularity, but their inability to perform core tasks competently undermines their professional credibility and the overall success of their team. Balancing warmth with competence is essential for building trust, and respect, and achieving sustainable success in any professional setting.

Putting it into Practice

- **Confidence in body language:** Project confidence through your body language. Maintain good posture, make eye contact, and use gestures purposefully. Stand or sit up straight, avoid fidgeting, and convey openness and assurance in your demeanour.

- **Speak with authority:** When communicating your ideas or expertise, speak with clarity, conviction, and authority. Use confident language, avoid filler words or hesitations, and articulate your points with conviction.

- **Demonstrate expertise:** Showcase your knowledge and expertise by providing well-researched and insightful contributions to discussions, presentations, or meetings. Share relevant examples, data, or case studies to support your arguments and demonstrate your depth of understanding.

- **Highlight achievements:** Highlight your past achievements, successes, and accomplishments to establish credibility and competence. Whether it's through a resume, portfolio, or LinkedIn profile, showcase your professional achievements and experiences to convey your competence to others. *(Remember! You have to avoid sounding boastful)*

- **Stay informed:** Stay updated with the latest industry trends, developments, and best practices relevant to your field. Regularly read industry publications, attend conferences or webinars, and engage in continuous learning to stay informed and demonstrate your commitment to professional growth.

- **Seek opportunities to lead:** Take on leadership roles or responsibilities within your organization or community to demonstrate your competence and ability to drive results. Lead projects, initiatives, or teams, and showcase your leadership skills through effective decision-making, problem-solving, and communication.

- **Provide solutions:** When faced with challenges or problems, approach them with a proactive mindset and focus on finding practical solutions. Demonstrate your ability to analyze problems, identify root causes, and develop effective strategies to address them, showcasing your competence in problem-solving.

- **Seek feedback and learn from mistakes:** Actively seek feedback from colleagues, supervisors, or mentors on your performance and areas for improvement. Embrace constructive criticism as an opportunity to learn and grow, and demonstrate your willingness to adapt and improve based on feedback received.

- **Collaborate effectively:** Demonstrate your competence in collaboration by effectively working with others to achieve shared goals or objectives. Communicate openly and transparently, listen actively to others' perspectives, and contribute constructively to team discussions and decisions.

- **Continuously improve:** Commit to ongoing self-improvement and professional development to enhance your competence over time. Set goals for skill development, seek out learning opportunities, and invest in training or education to continuously improve your knowledge, skills, and expertise.

We often meet people in our day-to-day lives both in personal and professional settings who are either high in warmth and low in competence or high in competence and low in warmth. Either of the categories is a hindrance in achieving your charismatic potential.

Words Have Power

Never underestimate the power of words. Using them effectively can help you tap into your charismatic potential. Words have the unique ability to shape perceptions, build connections, and influence outcomes. Research has shown that the language we use significantly impacts how others perceive us.

A study by Harvard University found that people who frequently use positive, confident language are perceived as more competent and likable. This means that the words you choose can either elevate or diminish your charisma.

Being positive in your language creates a welcoming and optimistic environment. Words of encouragement and appreciation uplift others and enhance your appeal. For instance, saying "Great job!" or "I appreciate your effort" fosters goodwill and respect.

Engaging in active listening and responding thoughtfully can make your interactions more meaningful. Phrases like "I understand how you feel" or "Tell me more about that" show empathy and genuine interest, which are key components of warmth.

By consciously choosing your words and focusing on clarity, positivity, and empathy, you can instantly elevate your charisma.

Warm Words	Competent Words
Support	Expertise
Understand	Intellectual
Kind	Proficient
Compassion	Talent
Care	Problem Solver
Encourage	Strategic
Grateful	Visionary

I hope this chapter helped you gain perspective on the importance of warmth and competence cues. You are now equipped with the knowledge of how using a perfect blend of warmth and charisma, you can tap into your highest charismatic potential

Key Takeaways

- **Charisma balance:** Charisma is the perfect blend of warmth (kindness, friendliness) and competence (skills, expertise), crucial for effective leadership and influence.
- **Impact of high competence, low warmth:** Individuals are respected but may be seen as intimidating or unapproachable, leading to fear among colleagues and low team morale.
- **Impact of high warmth, low competence:** Creates a positive and friendly environment but lacks professional credibility and effectiveness.

- **Importance of cues:** Verbal, nonverbal, and vocal cues influence perceptions, categorizing individuals as warm or competent.
- **Actionable tips:** Enhance warmth with sincere smiles, open body language, genuine interest, compliments, and gratitude. Improve competence through confident body language, authoritative speech, demonstrating expertise, highlighting achievements, and continuous learning.

Charisma Quiz: Calculate Your Charisma Score

Instructions: For each statement, check the response that best describes you. Use the following scale:

1. **Strongly Disagree (1 point)**
2. **Disagree (2 points)**
3. **Neutral (3 points)**
4. **Agree (4 points)**
5. **Strongly Agree (5 points)**

Let's start the quiz:

Statement	1	2	3	4	5
When I talk to someone, I make sure to give them my undivided attention.					
I feel confident and sure of myself in social situations.					
I often smile and use					

positive body language when interacting with others.					
I listen carefully to others without interrupting.					
I try to understand and relate to other people's feelings and perspectives.					
I prepare and organize my thoughts before speaking in important situations.					
I am aware of and control my body language to convey confidence.					
I am genuine and true to myself in interactions with others.					
I regularly seek and act on feedback to improve my social skills.					
People often come to me for advice and value my opinions.					

Scoring

Add up your scores for each question to get your total charisma score. Here's what your score means:

40-50: Highly Charismatic

You have a strong presence, are confident, and exude warmth. People are naturally drawn to you.

30-39: Moderately Charismatic

You have many charismatic qualities but **may** have a few areas to improve.

20-29: Developing Charisma

You have some charismatic traits but need to **work** on certain aspects to enhance your charisma.

10-19: Room for Improvement

You may struggle with charisma, but with focus and effort, you can develop these skills.

Use your score to identify areas where you can improve and work on enhancing your presence, power, and warmth to become more charismatic.

In the next chapter, we take a deep dive into the power of verbal cues in dialing up your charisma. Let's go...

Chapter 4

The Power of Words

Charisma is not about being the loudest voice in the room, but about speaking with intention and making every word count.
---- Simon Sinek

In 2013, on a reality TV dating show called 'Ready to Love', Matthew Hussey, a renowned dating and life coach, and best-selling author had his credibility at stake while being a judge on the show when a contestant attacked him when he tried to give her feedback.

Matthew expressed his views on the equation a female contestant shared with a male contestant on the show. He said, *"One thing that is clear about Ben is, he is someone who is extremely affectionate and he values someone who is really nurturing. Something that I haven't seen in you is the nurturing nature."* He added, *"When I watch you two, I always feel like you are on the brink of being able to argue about something."* He explains this with an instance he noticed during the show.

Matthew was in his late twenties *(still renowned for his work)* when this happened. This female contestant got offended and questioned his credibility saying sarcastically, *"How old are you, Matt?"* She further added, *"I am very sure that you are a self-proclaimed guru and I think most gurus are anything but a lot older. Especially in love, you need to have a tad too many years under your belt."*

When she was speaking, Matthew was silent the entire team, listening to her intently without interrupting her. He was calm during the entire situation and replied with just one sentence calmly when she finished, *"Tarryn, thanks for proving my point!"* And the entire room filled with the audience applauded.

Did you notice something in the above instance? Matthew was silent the entire time Tarryn was questioning him, his credibility, and his competence to be a judge of this show. Matthew let her complete and when he spoke, in one sentence he owned the room. The audience applauded when after his long pause and listening to everything Tarryn was saying, he chose just one sentence and got the upper hand in the situation that could have turned against him completely. When he said this in a calm and composed demeanour, he took all the power away from Tarryn's words which were blabbered in frustration. Further, he didn't act like he was trying to demean her with his words. He mentioned clearly that it was not personal and he was there just to help her. He behaved like a professional he is.

Now try to understand that this was on national television and the stakes were really high especially for Matthew in this situation because, one wrong move and he could have lost the credibility he had built over almost a decade of his career as an expert in men's behavior and a dating coach.

That is the power of your verbal cues. When used rightly, they can sparkle your personality with charisma but if not used right, they may create doubts about your credibility and authority. Especially if you are a teacher, your verbal cues are of utmost importance when you want to come across as charismatic and get the hold of the room you are in, be it in a classroom, a boardroom, a staffroom, or a parent-teacher meeting.

In this chapter, we will discuss what verbal cues are, the impact you can create when you use your verbal cues correctly, and how to use them to your advantage so that they add charisma to your personality.

What are verbal cues?

The words you use through spoken language that elicit a response from the listener are the 'verbal cues' you send.

Verbal cues are critical components of effective communication, serving several vital functions in both personal and professional interactions.

Firstly, verbal cues enhance clarity and understanding. Clear and precise language ensures that messages are conveyed accurately, reducing the potential for misunderstandings. For example, a teacher who says, *"Please submit your assignments by Friday at noon,"* provides specific instructions that students can easily follow, minimizing confusion.

Secondly, verbal cues play a crucial role in building and maintaining relationships. **Addressing individuals by name, giving compliments, and expressing appreciation** are verbal behaviors that demonstrate respect and recognition. This fosters a positive rapport and strengthens interpersonal connections in a classroom, workplace, or social setting. Thirdly, these cues are essential for encouraging engagement and participation. Questions, prompts, and invitations to contribute keep conversations dynamic and inclusive. In educational environments, teachers who ask, "What do you think about this idea?" or "Can someone share their perspective?" actively involve students, promoting critical thinking and active learning.

Furthermore, verbal cues can convey empathy and support, which are fundamental for building trust and emotional connections. Phrases like, **"I understand how you feel," or "I'm here to help,"** show that the speaker is attentive and compassionate, making the listener feel valued and understood.

Lastly, verbal cues project confidence and authority, enhancing the speaker's credibility. Using assertive language and speaking with conviction establishes a sense of competence and reliability.

Charismatic people hit a sweet spot for charisma by using a perfect blend of warm and competent words. Don't believe me? Let's do an activity.

Think of the 5 most charismatic people you know and write down their names:

1. ____

2. ____

3. ____

4. ____

5. ____

Open up the last five e-mails or texts you received from them. Note down the number of competent and warm words they use. Do you observe a pattern? In most cases, you would notice that they incorporate both, words signifying warmth and competence in their verbal cues.

In this chapter, I am going to take you through the six steps to craft your verbal cues to make your interactions charismatic and impactful:

#Step 1: Positive Reinforcement

Warm words are terms and phrases that convey kindness, empathy, and positivity. They help create a welcoming and supportive environment. Examples of warm words include- appreciate, understand, enjoy, thank you, glad, and great.

Impact on Students

The use of warm words has a significant psychological and emotional impact on students as proven by numerous studies.

As a teacher, when you use warm words, students feel valued and respected, which boosts their self-esteem and confidence. This positive reinforcement encourages a more engaging and participatory learning environment. For instance, when a teacher says, *"**Thank you for sharing,**"* it validates the student's contribution, making them feel heard and appreciated. Similarly, phrases like **"I'm glad you brought that up"** and **"That's a great point"** reinforce that students' opinions and thoughts are important, fostering a sense of belonging and motivation to contribute more actively in class.

Additionally, teachers should avoid using **'I'** language and instead use **'we'** to create a sense of unity and collaboration. For example, saying **"We can solve this together"** or **"Let's explore this idea"** makes students feel included and part of a team, enhancing their engagement and collective learning experience.

- **Express appreciation**: Use phrases like "Thank you for sharing" to acknowledge students' efforts and contributions. This shows that their input is valued.
- **Show understanding**: Incorporate phrases like "I understand how you feel" or "I appreciate your perspective" to demonstrate empathy and **validation** of students' emotions and viewpoints.
- **Encourage engagement**: Use phrases such as "I'm glad you brought that up" and "That's a great point" to foster an inclusive and interactive **classroom** environment. These statements encourage students to share their thoughts and ideas, knowing that their contributions are recognized and valued.

#Step 2: Crafting Competent Communication

Competent words are terms and phrases that convey expertise, knowledge, and professionalism. These words help establish a sense of authority and trust in the speaker. Examples of competent words include- analyze, evaluate, synthesize, assess, interpret, and deduce.

Using competent words in the classroom is crucial for establishing a teacher's credibility and authority. When you articulate your knowledge with precision and clarity, it reassures students of your expertise. This trust is foundational for effective teaching and learning.

For instance, when a teacher uses the word 'analyze,' it signals to students that they are being guided to think critically and deeply about a subject. When you use phrases like *"Based on my research..."* or *"According to the latest findings..."* demonstrate that your knowledge is rooted in evidence and ongoing learning, which further solidifies your authority.

Competent words also help in creating a structured and disciplined learning environment. When you consistently use language that reflects your expertise, it sets high academic standards and expectations for students. This motivates students to take their studies seriously and encourages them to strive for a deeper understanding of the subject matter.

Putting it into Practice

- **Express expertise**: Use phrases like 'based on my research' to indicate your knowledge is backed by thorough investigation and study. This reinforces your credibility and encourages students to respect and trust your insights.
- **Encourage critical thinking**: Incorporate terms like analyze, evaluate, and synthesize in your instructions and discussions. For example, instead of simply asking students to 'think about' a topic, ask them to 'analyze the underlying causes' or 'evaluate the effectiveness' of a concept or event.
- **Reference authority**: Use phrases such as 'According to the latest findings' to show that your teachings are up-to-date and aligned with current research. This demonstrates your ongoing commitment to learning and helps students understand the importance of staying informed and basing their knowledge on reliable sources.
- **Share experiences**: Use statements like 'In my experience' to connect theoretical knowledge with practical application. This helps students see the real-world relevance of what they are learning and builds trust in your practical expertise.

#Step 3: Power Phrases

Encouraging and positive language involves using words and phrases that uplift, motivate, and support students. This language style is essential for creating a classroom atmosphere where students feel valued, capable, and motivated to learn. Positive reinforcement helps build students' self-esteem, resilience, and willingness to engage in the learning process. By focusing on their strengths and potential, teachers can foster a growth mindset, encouraging students to view challenges as opportunities for growth.

Positive language plays a crucial role in motivating and inspiring students. When you use affirming words, students are more likely to feel confident and motivated to take on challenges. For instance, phrases like **"You can do it"** or **"I believe in you"** instill a sense of self-efficacy and determination, making students more likely to persist through difficulties. Additionally, recognizing and praising effort rather than just outcomes helps students understand the value of hard work and persistence. This approach not only motivates students to keep trying but also helps them develop a love for learning and a positive attitude toward their educational journey.

Putting it into Practice

- **Affirm belief**: Use phrases such as 'You can do it' and 'I believe in you' to show students that you have confidence in their abilities. This boosts their self-confidence and motivates them to persevere through challenges.
- **Praise effort**: Acknowledge students' hard work and persistence with phrases like 'Keep up the good work.' This reinforces positive behaviors and encourages students to continue striving for improvement.
- **Reframe negativity**: Avoid using negative phrases. Instead of saying 'That's wrong,' reframe it positively by saying, 'Let's try this approach.' This keeps the focus on finding solutions and encourages

a mindset oriented toward problem-solving and learning from mistakes.

#Step 4: Personalization

Addressing students by their names is a simple yet powerful tool for personalization in the classroom. It demonstrates that you recognize and value each student as an individual. Using a student's name in conversation can significantly enhance their sense of belonging and importance within the classroom community. This small act of acknowledgment helps students feel seen and respected, which can positively impact their engagement and motivation to participate in class activities.

Using students' names is a fundamental way to build personal connections and trust. When you address students by name, it creates a more intimate and caring classroom environment. This practice helps foster a sense of security and trust, making students more likely to open up, ask questions, and express their thoughts without fear of being overlooked. **Trust** is crucial for effective learning, as it encourages students to take risks, make mistakes, and learn from them. When students feel that their teacher knows them personally, they are more likely to develop a positive attitude toward the teacher and the learning process.

Putting it into Practice

- **Learn and use names regularly**: Make it a priority to learn all students' names as quickly as possible. Use their names in daily interactions, whether during roll call, in casual conversations, or while addressing them in class. This shows students that you see them as individuals and care about their presence in your class.
- **Incorporate names in feedback**: Use students' names when giving both positive feedback and constructive criticism. For example, saying

"Great job on your project, Sarah" or "Rahul, let's work on improving your essay's structure" makes the feedback feel more personal and directed. This approach helps students feel directly engaged and more likely to pay attention to the feedback being given.

#Step 5: Specific is Terrific

Selecting the right words involves balancing the use of subject-specific terminology with clear, accessible language. This approach helps in establishing your credibility while also making the content understandable for all students. **Over-explaining** can lead to information overload and confusion, so it's important to use vocabulary that is precise and appropriate for the students' level of comprehension.

Finding the right balance between providing enough information and over-explaining is crucial in maintaining student engagement and comprehension. When you over-explain, you are at a risk of overwhelming students with unnecessary details, which can lead to confusion and disengagement. On the other hand, insufficient information can leave students feeling unsure and unable to grasp the concepts fully. Therefore,it's important to strike a balance where students receive sufficient information to understand the topic without feeling overloaded.

Putting it into Practice

- **Use appropriate academic vocabulary**: Employ vocabulary that is relevant to the subject matter and suited to the students' academic level. For instance, in a science class, use terms like "hypothesis," "experiment," and "analysis," but ensure that students understand these terms through clear definitions and context.
- **Avoid unnecessary jargon**: While it's important to introduce subject-specific terminology, avoid using jargon that may be

unfamiliar or confusing to students unless it's essential for understanding the topic. When jargon is necessary, provide clear explanations and examples to help students grasp the meaning.

- **Break down complex information**: Divide complex topics into smaller, digestible parts. Present each part clearly and check for student understanding before moving on to the next point.

- **Use questions to gauge understanding**: Before elaborating further, use questions to assess students' comprehension. This helps teachers gauge how much detail is necessary and where additional explanation may be needed.

- **Encourage student questions**: Encourage students to ask questions throughout the lesson. This allows teachers to tailor their explanations to meet students' needs and interests, ensuring that the information provided is relevant and engaging.

#Step 6: Self-Reflection

Effective verbal communication is a cornerstone of creating a positive and engaging classroom environment. As a teacher, it's crucial to regularly reflect on your current use of verbal cues to ensure they are fostering student engagement and motivation. Begin by considering the following questions:

1. **Warm Words and Encouraging Language**:
   - Am I using warm words and encouraging language to create a supportive atmosphere?
   - How often do I address students by their names during interactions?
2. **Competent Words and Appropriate Vocabulary**:
   - Do I consistently use competent words and appropriate academic vocabulary?

- ○ Am I balancing clarity and precision in my explanations without over-explaining?

3. **Effectiveness of Verbal Cues**:
   - ○ Are my verbal cues effectively motivating students and promoting active participation?
   - ○ Do I adjust my communication based on student responses and engagement levels?

Seek Feedback and Improvement

Seeking feedback from students and colleagues is essential for improving your verbal communication skills in the classroom. Students can provide valuable insights into what encourages and motivates them, while colleagues can offer constructive feedback and suggestions for improvement. Consider the following strategies:

- **Student Feedback**: Create opportunities for students to provide anonymous feedback on your communication style. Ask them specific questions about how they feel about your use of warm words, competent language, and addressing them by name.
- **Colleague Feedback**: Engage in peer observation sessions where colleagues can provide feedback on your verbal cues during classroom interactions. Collaborate with colleagues to exchange strategies and ideas for improving communication skills.
  - **Monitoring and Reflection**:
    - ○ Regularly monitor your progress towards your goals.
    - ○ Reflect on the effectiveness of your verbal cues and make adjustments as needed.
    - ○ Seek ongoing feedback from students and colleagues to refine your communication strategies.

By implementing this action plan, you will enhance your ability to use verbal cues effectively, creating a more supportive, engaging, and motivating classroom environment for your students.

By continually refining your verbal cues, you will not only become a more charismatic and effective educator but also create a classroom environment where students feel respected, motivated, and inspired to learn.

Let's Analyze your Verbal Cues

Have you ever thought about how effectively are you communicating your charisma through your verbal cues? Let's do an audit of your verbal cues.

Review all your assets in the table given below and count the number of warm and competent words you use. This will help you identify your dominant side and help you understand whether you need to use more warmth cues or competent cues.

	Warm Words	Competent Words
LinkedIn Profile		
Voicemail		
E-mail Signature		
Your last ten social media posts		
Business cards for marketing material		

(This exercise is adapted from the book *Cues* by Vanessa Van Edwards.)

<h1 style="text-align:center">Key Takeaways</h1>

- **Verbal cues** such as warm words, competent language, and encouraging phrases are powerful tools for building a positive classroom environment.
- **Addressing students by their names** helps to establish personal connections and fosters a sense of respect and belonging.
- **Using appropriate vocabulary** and avoiding over-explanation ensures clarity and maintains student engagement.
- **Positive language** and encouragement motivate students, boost their confidence, and encourage active participation.
- **Reflect** on and refine your use of verbal cues through self-assessment and feedback from students and colleagues to enhance teaching effectiveness.

In the next chapter, we'll dive deeper into becoming the charismatic teacher you're meant to be by unlocking the power that lies within. And no, I'm not talking about the power of speaking. Stay tuned to discover what it truly is!

Chapter 5

Speaking Without Words

Charisma is the intangible that makes people want to follow you, to be around you, to be influenced by you.

--- Roger Dawson

People naturally respond to the signals your body sends out. Why is this important? Think about it: in both your personal and professional life, you've likely encountered someone and instantly sensed their mood or formed an initial impression without exchanging a single word. Why does this happen? It's because of the **non-verbal cues** they project, revealing their state of mind.

What are non-verbal cues?

Non-verbal cues are the expressions and mannerisms we use to communicate non-verbally. This includes our physical behaviour which is intuitive rather than conscious. Whenever you interact with others, your gestures and postures are sending non-verbal messages to the person you interact with. Even when you are silent, you are still communicating nonverbally through your body.

The research underscores the profound impact of non-verbal communication on the overall communication process. According to Albert Mehrabian's communication model, **55% of communication is conveyed through body language, 38% through vocal elements such as tone and pitch, and a mere 7% through actual words.** This highlights the critical importance of non-verbal cues in shaping perceptions and facilitating understanding.

Furthermore, studies have demonstrated that effective use of non-verbal communication can significantly enhance teaching outcomes, improve student engagement, and foster stronger teacher-student rapport. By being mindful of non-verbal signals, educators can cultivate a more dynamic and responsive classroom environment.

Components of Body Language

Let's delve into five key components of body language: **posture, movement, hand gestures, eye contact, and facial expressions.**

- ★ Posture reveals confidence and openness or discomfort and defensiveness.
- ★ Movement, whether purposeful or nervous, communicates confidence or anxiety.
- ★ Hand gestures enhance verbal communication, conveying specific messages or emotional states.
- ★ Eye contact establishes interest, confidence, or discomfort and plays a crucial role in building trust.
- ★ Facial expressions universally convey emotions like happiness, surprise, or anxiety, significantly impacting interactions.

Understanding these elements will help improve personal and professional communication, making interactions more effective and meaningful.
Let's explore each of these components in depth.

Posture

Posture refers to the way **an individual positions their body while sitting, standing, or moving**. It plays a crucial role in non-verbal communication, often conveying messages about a person's confidence, openness, attentiveness, and overall emotional state. Good posture can enhance one's presence and influence in social interactions, while poor posture can detract from it.

Examples of Different Postures and Their Meanings

1. **Open vs. Closed Posture**
   - **Open Posture:** This involves standing or sitting with arms relaxed and uncrossed, feet flat on the ground or slightly apart, and the torso exposed. Open posture is generally associated with openness, confidence, and a willingness to engage. It makes the person appear approachable and receptive. For example, a manager standing with hands by their sides and facing employees during a meeting conveys openness to ideas and discussion.
   - **Closed Posture:** This includes crossing arms or legs, turning away slightly, or hunching over. Closed posture typically signals defensiveness, discomfort, or lack of interest. For instance, a person crossing their arms and legs while sitting in a meeting may seem defensive or disengaged from the discussion.
2. **Erect vs. Slouched Posture**
   - **Erect Posture:** Standing or sitting upright with shoulders back and head held high signals confidence, attentiveness, and readiness. An erect posture is often perceived as a sign of authority and competence. For example, a speaker standing

upright while delivering a presentation appears more confident and engaging.

- ○ **Slouched Posture:** Slumping, leaning back excessively, or letting the shoulders droop indicates a lack of interest, low energy, or low self-esteem. In a professional setting, a slouched posture can be interpreted as disengagement or lack of confidence. For example, a student slumping in their chair during a lecture may appear uninterested or tired.

Research Findings on Posture and Its Impact on Perception

Research has shown that posture significantly affects how individuals are perceived and how they perceive themselves. One notable study by social psychologist Amy Cuddy explored the concept of '**power posing**'. In her research, participants who adopted high-power poses (*e.g., standing with hands on hips and feet apart*) for a few minutes experienced increases in testosterone levels and decreases in cortisol levels. These hormonal changes were linked to increased feelings of power and risk tolerance. Conversely, participants who adopted low-power poses (e.g., sitting with arms wrapped around themselves) experienced opposite hormonal changes and reported feeling less confident and more stressed.

The implications of these findings suggest that adopting confident, open postures can not only change how others perceive us but also how we perceive ourselves. This is particularly relevant in high-stakes situations like job interviews, presentations, or negotiations, where projecting confidence can significantly impact outcomes. For instance, someone going into a job interview might benefit from spending a few minutes in a high-power pose beforehand to boost their confidence and performance.

Movement

Movement in body language **refers to the various ways in which individuals move their bodies, including gestures, walking, shifting weight, and other physical actions.** Movements can convey a range of emotions and intentions, from confidence and decisiveness to nervousness and anxiety. The significance of movement lies in its ability to complement or contradict verbal communication, thereby reinforcing or undermining the messages being conveyed. Effective use of movement can enhance communication by making it more dynamic and engaging.

Examples of Purposeful vs. Nervous Movements

1. **Purposeful Movements:** These are deliberate and controlled actions that convey confidence and authority. Purposeful movements include:
   - **Walking Confidently:** Moving with a steady pace, head held high, and shoulders back. For example, a business leader walking into a room with a confident stride can immediately command attention and respect.
   - **Deliberate Gestures:** Using hand and arm movements intentionally to emphasize points during a conversation or presentation. For instance, a speaker who uses open hand gestures to illustrate their points appears more engaging and confident.
   - **Controlled Movements:** Maintaining steady and smooth motions, such as moving calmly between different areas of a room while speaking, which signals composure and authority.
2. **Nervous Movements:** These are involuntary or erratic actions that often indicate anxiety, discomfort, or lack of confidence. Nervous movements include:

- ○ **Fidgeting:** Playing with objects, tapping fingers, or repeatedly adjusting clothing. For example, someone who constantly fidgets with a pen during a meeting may be perceived as anxious or distracted.

- ○ **Shifting Weight Frequently:** Moving from foot to foot, swaying, or frequently changing posture. This can signal unease or nervousness, as seen in a person who shifts their weight back and forth while speaking in front of a group.

- ○ **Pacing:** Walking back and forth repeatedly without a clear purpose can indicate anxiety or agitation, such as a student pacing nervously before giving a presentation.

Research Findings on Movement and its Impact on Communication

Research has demonstrated that movement significantly affects how messages are received and interpreted. One notable study on public speaking effectiveness found that **purposeful movement can enhance a speaker's credibility and audience engagement.** In this study, speakers who moved confidently and used deliberate gestures were rated more positively by their audiences compared to those who remained static or exhibited nervous movements.

The study highlighted that movement can serve as a powerful tool to keep audiences engaged and reinforce verbal messages. For example, speakers who use strategic movement to shift focus or emphasize key points can create a more dynamic and memorable presentation. Conversely, excessive or erratic movements can distract the audience and detract from the speaker's message.

Hand Gestures

Hand gestures are **deliberate movements of the hands and arms used to convey messages or support verbal communication.** They are significant because they can enhance clarity, emphasize points, and provide visual cues that reinforce spoken words. Hand gestures help convey emotions and intentions, making communication more dynamic and engaging. They can bridge language barriers and add a layer of meaning that words alone might not fully capture.

Examples of Different Types of Hand Gestures and Their Meanings

1. **Emblematic Gestures:** These are culturally specific hand movements that convey specific, well-understood messages. Examples include:
   - **Thumbs Up:** Universally recognized as a sign of approval or agreement.
   - **Waving:** Used as a greeting or farewell gesture.
   - **Peace Sign:** A gesture signifying peace or victory.

Emblematic gestures are direct substitutes for words and are understood without verbal accompaniment. *For instance, a thumbs-up in a meeting can instantly indicate agreement or support without interrupting the speaker.*

2. **Illustrative Gestures:** These gestures accompany speech and are used to illustrate or reinforce the verbal message. Examples include:
   - **Describing Size or Shape:** Using hands to indicate the size of an object, such as spreading hands apart to show something large.
   - **Directional Movements:** Pointing or using sweeping motions to indicate direction or flow.

- ○ **Pacing Gestures:** Moving hands rhythmically to match the cadence of speech, which helps emphasize points and make the speech more engaging.

Illustrative gestures help the audience visualize concepts and can make explanations clearer. *For example, a teacher describing a mountain might use hand gestures to outline its shape, enhancing students' understanding.*

3. **Adaptive Gestures:** These are self-touching behaviors that often indicate personal needs or emotional states. Examples include:
   - ○ **Scratching:** May indicate discomfort or nervousness.
   - ○ **Tapping Fingers:** Often a sign of impatience or anxiety.
   - ○ **Playing with Objects:** Such as twisting a ring or fiddling with a pen, which can signal stress or distraction.

Adaptive gestures are usually subconscious and can reveal underlying feelings that might not be expressed verbally. Recognizing these can provide insight into a person's emotional state during a conversation.

Research Findings on Hand Gestures and Their Role in Enhancing Communication

Research has shown that hand gestures play a crucial role in enhancing communication by improving memory retention and comprehension. One notable study by **Dr. Susan Goldin-Meadow from the University of Chicago found that gestures can significantly enhance learning and memory.** In her research, participants who used hand gestures while learning new concepts had better recall and understanding of the material compared to those who did not use gestures.

The study highlighted that gestures help encode information in memory by engaging multiple cognitive processes. For example, when a speaker uses illustrative gestures to describe a concept, it creates a visual representation that complements the verbal message. This dual encoding (visual and verbal) strengthens memory retention and makes it easier for the audience to understand and recall the information later.

Hand gestures are a vital component of non-verbal communication that can significantly enhance the clarity and impact of verbal messages.

Eye Contact

Eye contact **refers to the act of looking directly into another person's eyes during a conversation.** It is a powerful form of non-verbal communication that conveys a wide range of emotions and intentions. Eye contact can indicate interest, confidence, attentiveness, and honesty. It is crucial in building rapport, establishing trust, and facilitating effective interpersonal communication. Proper use of eye contact can enhance the clarity and impact of a message, making interactions more engaging and meaningful.

Examples of Different Types of Eye Contact and Their Meanings

1. **Direct Eye Contact:**
   - Definition: Direct eye contact involves looking straight into someone's eyes while speaking or listening.
   - Meaning: Direct eye contact usually indicates interest, confidence, and attentiveness. It shows that the person is engaged in the conversation and values what the other person is saying. In many cultures, it is also a sign of honesty and respect. For instance, in a job interview, maintaining direct eye contact can convey confidence and sincerity, making a positive impression on the interviewer.

2. **Avoiding Eye Contact:**
   - Definition: Avoiding eye contact involves looking away or down instead of making eye contact.
   - Meaning: Avoiding eye contact can indicate discomfort, shyness, or evasiveness. It may suggest that the person is anxious, lacks confidence, or is trying to hide something. For example, a student avoiding eye contact with a teacher while being questioned might be nervous or unsure of the answer. In some cultures, however, avoiding eye contact can be a sign of respect, particularly towards elders or authority figures.
3. **Prolonged Eye Contact:**
   - Definition: Prolonged eye contact refers to maintaining eye contact for an extended period, often to the point of staring.
   - Meaning: Prolonged eye contact can indicate dominance, aggression, or intense interest. While maintaining eye contact is generally positive, staring can make others feel uncomfortable or threatened. For instance, in a negotiation, prolonged eye contact can be used to assert dominance or pressure the other party. However, it can also be perceived as aggressive or confrontational if not balanced with natural breaks.

Research Findings on Eye Contact and its Impact on Perception and Interaction

Research has extensively studied the role of eye contact in communication, revealing its significant impact on perception and interaction. A notable study by **Dr. Michael Argyle and Janet Dean at the University of Oxford explored how eye contact influences social behavior.** They found that eye contact is a critical factor in establishing trust and rapport. Their research showed that people who make appropriate eye contact are perceived as more trustworthy, likable, and competent.

Another study conducted by researchers at the University of Wolverhampton examined the role of eye contact in building connections and facilitating social interactions. The study found that mutual eye contact activates the brain's social cognition network, making individuals feel more connected and understood. This neural activation helps create a sense of empathy and bonding, which is essential for effective communication.

Eye contact also plays a vital role in regulating conversational flow. Research by Dr. Adam Kendon highlighted that speakers often use eye contact to signal their intention to continue or finish speaking, while listeners use it to indicate attention and readiness to respond. This non-verbal cue helps manage turn-taking in conversations, ensuring smooth and effective communication.

In the context of establishing authority, eye contact can significantly impact how a person is perceived. **Studies have shown that leaders who maintain strong eye contact are seen as more authoritative and confident.** Conversely, those who avoid eye contact may be perceived as less confident or evasive, potentially undermining their credibility and influence.

Facial Expressions

Facial expressions **are movements or positions of the facial muscles that convey emotional states, intentions, and reactions.** They are a vital aspect of non-verbal communication, providing immediate visual cues about a person's feelings and reactions. Unlike words, which can be controlled and manipulated, facial expressions often reveal true emotions, making them a reliable indicator of one's internal state. The ability to read and interpret facial expressions is crucial for effective interpersonal communication, as it helps individuals respond appropriately to others' emotions and intentions.In the next chapter, we'll dive deeper into becoming the charismatic teacher you're meant to be by unlocking the power that lies within. And no, I'm not talking about the power of speaking. Stay tuned to discover what it truly is!

Examples of Common Facial Expressions and Their Meanings

1. **Smiling:**
   - Definition: A smile involves the upward turning of the corners of the mouth and often includes crinkling around the eyes.
   - Meaning: Smiling generally indicates happiness, friendliness, and approachability. It is a universal signal of positive emotion. For example, smiling during a conversation can make the other person feel welcomed and appreciated, fostering a positive interaction.

2. **Frowning:**
   - Definition: A frown is characterized by the downward turning of the corners of the mouth and furrowing of the brow.
   - Meaning: Frowning can indicate displeasure, confusion, or concentration. It is often a sign that something is wrong or that a person is deeply focused. For instance, a student frowning during a lecture might be struggling to understand the material or may be unhappy with the topic.

3. **Raised Eyebrows:**
   - Definition: Raising the eyebrows involves lifting them upward, often widening the eyes.
   - Meaning: Raised eyebrows can indicate surprise, interest, or skepticism. This expression helps convey a reaction to unexpected information or an emotion of disbelief. For

example, raised eyebrows during a meeting might show surprise at a new idea or skepticism about a proposal.

4. **Lip Biting:**
   ○ Definition: Lip biting involves gently biting the lower lip with the upper teeth.
   ○ Meaning: Lip biting can indicate anxiety or uncertainty. It is a common self-soothing gesture when a person is nervous or unsure. For example, someone biting their lip during a presentation might be feeling anxious about speaking in public or uncertain about their performance.

Research Findings on Facial Expressions and their Role in Conveying Emotions

The significance of facial expressions in conveying emotions has been extensively researched. **One of the most notable researchers in this field is Paul Ekman, who conducted pioneering studies on universal facial expressions.** Ekman and his colleagues identified six basic emotions—*happiness, sadness, anger, fear, surprise, and disgust*—that are universally recognized across cultures through facial expressions. His research demonstrated that despite cultural differences, people around the world use similar facial expressions to convey these fundamental emotions.

Ekman's studies involved showing participants from various cultures photographs of faces expressing different emotions and asking them to identify the emotions. The results showed high agreement among participants from different cultural backgrounds, supporting the idea that certain facial expressions are biologically hardwired and universally understood.

Further research has highlighted the role of facial expressions in social interactions.

Next, we explore how to exude charisma from the very moment you introduce yourself, step onto a stage, or even say your first 'Hello.'

Charismatic First Impressions

They say, "First impression is the last impression," but I disagree. Our perceptions of people can change over time as we get to know them. However, there's no denying that first impressions are powerful and hard to change if they go wrong. It's better to make a good first impression, but even if you don't, it's possible to recover. The effort required depends on the initial damage done.

We've all botched first impressions, whether in an important boardroom meeting or on the first day at a new job. Yet, with the right approach, you can repair and even completely transform the initial perception. Let me share a personal story from my experience as a teacher, where my first impression was far from perfect. But I turned it around. Curious how? Keep reading to find out.

Let's take a journey back to the early 2000s. In a prestigious school in Mumbai, I embarked on the first day of my teaching career. Securing this position was beyond my expectations, as the institution catered to an elite clientele with students from affluent backgrounds. Landing such a coveted role at the beginning of my career felt like a dream come true. The significance of this opportunity was immense for me, as it marked my ideal entry into the world of education. My happiness was palpable, and I felt as though nothing could erase the smile from my face. Little did I know that in mere moments, I would be wiping away tears with my dupatta.

I entered the grade 5 classroom with a mixture of excitement and nervousness. My heart was pounding, as this was my first time facing a group of fifth-grade students who, in my view, were far more street-smart than I was at the time. Despite being their teacher, I felt an overwhelming sense of inferiority, convinced they were superior to me. Determined to set aside this inferiority complex and establish rapport, I began my lesson. However, my feelings of inadequacy, fear, and self-doubt soon overtook me. In that moment, my non-verbal cues were chaotic and betrayed my inner turmoil. **My posture was poor, my hand gestures were hesitant and shrinking, my voice was subdued, and my eye contact was lacking.** My turbulent emotions became evident, and my body language unmistakably conveyed my lack of confidence.

The children in the class seized the moment, sensing they could dominate me. They disregarded my instructions and seemed to reject a teacher who lacked authority. As time passed, I lost control of the entire class. The situation became so chaotic that I had no choice but to walk out. In hindsight, I realize it was my first encounter with the profound impact of non-verbal communication. Reflecting on that day, I understand I could have exuded confidence and spoken with clarity while maintaining a smile or a firm demeanor. I could have projected authority through my body language while also conveying warmth.

The signals I conveyed that day suggested I had warmth but lacked competence, which worked against me. It was disheartening, especially since I had meticulously prepared. As someone who thrives on preparation before any significant event, I had rehearsed my speech to the students extensively. Yet, everything unraveled on 'the day.' Feeling miserable about making a poor first impression on my students, I spent considerable time reflecting on and analyzing the situation. I was determined to persevere and not quit my job.

The next day, I mustered more courage and returned to the classroom. At the time, I wasn't aware that my body language needed improvement. Determined to recover, I reminded myself that lamenting over past mistakes was futile. Entering the class with renewed confidence, I divided the students into small groups and engaged with them individually, building rapport. Gradually, I won the class over.

This transformation took about a month and required significant effort. The initial misstep was due to my inadequate non-verbal communication, but through persistence and adjustment, I earned the students' acceptance as their teacher.

Reflecting on my first day of teaching underscores the critical role of non-verbal communication in establishing authority and rapport. Scientific research, including **Albert Mehrabian's model, shows that 93%** of effective communication is non-verbal, with body language and tone of voice being key. My initial insecurity and lack of confidence undermined my words, causing a loss of control in the classroom. However, by adjusting my non-verbal cues, I regained presence and earned students' respect.

While a first impression isn't the last, it does leave a lasting impact. Changing a negative impression is possible but challenging. Instead, master a few basic principles to make a powerful first impression from the start.

Putting it into Practice

- **Stand tall:** Maintain an erect posture to convey confidence and authority.
- **Smile genuinely:** A warm, genuine smile can make you appear approachable and friendly.
- **Make eye contact:** Engage in direct eye contact to show interest and build trust.
- **Use purposeful gestures:** Employ deliberate hand gestures to emphasize key points and demonstrate control.
- **Dress appropriately:** Wear attire that balances professionalism and approachability to enhance your credibility.
- **Speak clearly:** Use a strong, clear voice to project confidence and ensure your message is understood.
- **Pause effectively:** Incorporate pauses to allow students to process information and to highlight important points.
- **Show enthusiasm:** Express genuine enthusiasm and passion for the subject to engage and motivate students.
- **Be prepared:** Familiarize yourself with the material to reduce anxiety and demonstrate competence.
- **Listen actively:** Show attentiveness to students' responses and feedback, making them feel valued and respected.

Strategies for Teachers to create a Charismatic First Impression in Various Situations

In the Classroom

1. Prepare Thoroughly: Before entering the classroom, ensure you have a solid understanding of the material and have prepared engaging activities or discussions. Being well-prepared helps reduce anxiety and boosts confidence.

2. Enter with Confidence: Walk into the classroom with an erect posture, head held high, and a genuine smile. This body language exudes confidence and sets a positive tone.

3. Establish Eye Contact: Make direct eye contact with your students as you greet them. Eye contact shows that you are engaged and interested in them, helping to build trust and rapport.

4. Use Open Body Language: Avoid crossing your arms or slouching. Instead, use open and expansive gestures. Open body language indicates approachability and confidence.

5. Speak Clearly and Audibly: Ensure your voice is loud enough to be heard by all students. Speak clearly and at a moderate pace, emphasizing key points with deliberate pauses.

6. Show Enthusiasm: Express genuine enthusiasm for the subject matter. Passion is contagious and can significantly boost student engagement.

7. Engage Students from the Start: Begin with an interesting question, a thought-provoking quote, or a relevant story. This captures students' attention and piques their interest right away.

8. Personalize Your Approach: Learn and use students' names as quickly as possible. Personalization makes students feel valued and more connected to you.

9. Use Humor Wisely: A touch of appropriate humor can lighten the mood and make you more relatable. However, ensure that it is suitable for the classroom environment.

10. Be Attentive and Responsive: Listen actively to students' questions and feedback. Showing that you value their input helps build a positive relationship from the start.

In Meetings

1. Arrive Early: Arriving early demonstrates punctuality and gives you time to settle in and compose yourself before the meeting begins.

2. Greet Everyone Warmly: Greet colleagues and participants with a firm handshake, eye contact, and a warm smile. This establishes immediate rapport.

3. Display Confident Body Language: Sit or stand with good posture, avoid fidgeting, and use open gestures. Confident body language helps convey your authority and ease.

4. Listen Actively: Show that you are paying attention by nodding, making eye contact, and providing verbal acknowledgments like "I see" or "That's interesting."

5. Speak with Clarity and Purpose: When it's your turn to speak, articulate your points clearly and concisely. Use a confident tone and modulate your volume to emphasize key points.

6. Be Prepared: Come prepared with all necessary materials and a clear understanding of the agenda. Preparation reduces nervousness and enhances your credibility.

7. Engage in Constructive Dialogue: Encourage a collaborative atmosphere by asking thoughtful questions and being open to others' ideas and perspectives.

8. Use Positive Facial Expressions: Smile, maintain a pleasant facial expression, and avoid looking distracted or bored. Positive expressions foster a welcoming environment.

9. Manage Nervous Habits: Be aware of and try to minimize any nervous habits like tapping your foot or playing with a pen, as these can be distracting.

10. Follow Up: After the meeting, follow up with a summary or thank-you email. This reinforces your professionalism and keeps the lines of communication open.

While Networking

1. Approach with Confidence: Approach new contacts with a confident stride, a smile, and a firm handshake. Confidence is key in making a strong first impression.

2. Introduce Yourself Effectively: Have a brief, engaging introduction ready. Mention your name, your role, and something interesting or relevant to the event.

3. Be an Active Listener: Show genuine interest in others by listening actively, maintaining eye contact, and asking follow-up questions.

4. Use Open Body Language: Keep your body language open and welcoming. Avoid crossing your arms and face the person you are speaking to directly.

5. Share Your Passion: Speak about your interests and professional passions with enthusiasm. Passion is contagious and can leave a lasting impression.

6. Be Mindful of Your Tone: Use a friendly and warm tone. Avoid sounding overly formal or too casual.

7. Exchange Contact Information: Have business cards ready and offer them after a meaningful interaction. This makes it easier to continue the conversation later.

8. Follow Up Promptly: Send a follow-up email or message within a day or two to thank them for the conversation and suggest ways to keep in touch.

9. Be Respectful of Time: Be concise in your conversations and mindful of the other person's time. This shows respect and professionalism.

10. Be Yourself: Authenticity goes a long way. Be genuine in your interactions, and people will appreciate.

Interpreting Students' Body Language Signals

Reading students' body language is crucial for us as educators to gauge their engagement and understanding in the classroom. This skill allows teachers to adjust their teaching methods accordingly, ensuring effective communication and learning outcomes.

1. **Common Signs of Student Engagement:** Engaged students display various non-verbal cues that indicate their interest and involvement in the lesson. These include leaning forward in their seats, nodding in agreement or understanding, maintaining eye contact with the teacher or peers, and actively participating in discussions. According to educational research, these behaviors signal that students are paying attention and are mentally focused on the content being presented.

2. **Signs of Disengagement or Boredom:** On the other hand, signs of student disengagement or boredom can be observed through different non-verbal cues. These may include slouching or leaning back in their seats, avoiding eye contact with the teacher, peers, or the lesson materials, fidgeting with objects or their hands, and frequently looking at the clock or around the room. These behaviors indicate that students may be distracted, uninterested, or find the material challenging.

3. **Recognizing Confusion and Understanding:** Recognizing when students are confused or unsure is essential for effective teaching. Body language cues that indicate confusion often include furrowed brows, squinting eyes, a tilted head, or a puzzled expression. These signals suggest that students are grappling with the material or need further clarification.

4. **Signals that Show Comprehension and Interest:** Conversely, when students understand the material and are interested in the lesson, they may display different non-verbal cues. These can include nodding in agreement or understanding, maintaining eye contact with the teacher or peers, taking notes actively, and occasionally smiling or showing signs of excitement. These behaviors suggest that students are comprehending the content and are engaged in the learning process.

Being able to read these cues allows teachers to adjust their teaching strategies to better meet students' needs. For instance, noticing signs of confusion may prompt the teacher to provide additional explanations or examples, while recognizing signs of comprehension can affirm that the lesson is effectively meeting its objectives.

Managing Behavioral Issues Using Body Language

Identifying signs of potential behavioral problems in students is crucial for maintaining a positive classroom environment. These signs can manifest in various forms, such as crossing arms, glaring, restlessness, and other non-verbal displays of aggression or discomfort. Such behaviors often indicate underlying issues such as frustration, defiance, anxiety, or a lack of engagement with the material being presented

To manage these situations effectively, teachers can employ strategies to de-escalate tension and redirect student behavior using body language.

★ One effective approach is to adopt a calm and neutral **posture**. This can include standing or sitting with an open body stance, keeping arms uncrossed, and maintaining appropriate eye contact. These behaviors convey empathy and a willingness to listen, without escalating the situation further.

★ **Movement and proximity** can also be used strategically. Moving closer to a student while maintaining a non-threatening posture can demonstrate support and encourage the student to communicate their feelings. This approach can help to diffuse tension and make the student feel more comfortable and understood.

★ Additionally, **mirroring** the student's body language subtly can help establish rapport and defuse hostility. For example, if a student is sitting with crossed arms, the teacher can mirror this posture briefly before adopting a more open stance, signaling a willingness to empathize with the student's feelings.

These body language techniques allow teachers to address behavioral issues promptly and constructively.

Putting it into Practice

- **Observe posture**: Note if students are sitting upright, indicating engagement, or slouching, indicating disinterest.
- **Watch eye contact**: Pay attention to whether students are making eye contact or avoiding it, as this can signal attention or discomfort.
- **Monitor facial expressions**: Look for smiles, furrowed brows, or blank stares to gauge understanding and emotions.
- **Notice gestures**: Observe hand-raising, note-taking, or fidgeting to assess participation and focus.
- **Identify physical proximity**: Students leaning forward may be more engaged, while those leaning back or away may be disengaged.
- **Track movements**: Note if students are restless or frequently moving, which can indicate boredom or anxiety.
- **Check head positioning**: A tilted head can indicate curiosity or confusion, while a downturned head may suggest disengagement.
- **Recognize patterns**: Look for recurring non-verbal cues that consistently indicate a student's engagement level.
- **Acknowledge group dynamics**: Observe how students interact with peers, which can influence individual body language.
- **Adapt teaching strategies**: Adjust your approach based on observed body language to better meet students' needs.

Appearance as a Non-Verbal Cue

Appearance is a powerful form of non-verbal communication that significantly influences first impressions. The way teachers present themselves can convey confidence, professionalism, and approachability without uttering a single word. Elements such as attire, grooming, and overall presentation play crucial roles in establishing authority and setting the tone in educational environments. By carefully considering their appearance, teachers can enhance their credibility, foster respect, and create a positive and welcoming atmosphere for students and colleagues alike.

The Importance of Appearance in Non-Verbal Communication for Teachers

Non-verbal communication, including appearance, plays a crucial role in educational settings. Appearance—encompassing attire, grooming, and personal hygiene—affects perceptions of professionalism, authority, and trustworthiness.

Research by Birchmeier (2011) indicates that teachers who dress professionally are viewed more positively by students and are seen as more credible and authoritative. This perception enhances other non-verbal cues like eye contact, facial expressions, and body language, which are vital for building rapport and managing classroom dynamics.

Additionally, studies by Hall and Jones (2000) show that students respect teachers who adhere to professional dress codes, which fosters a positive classroom climate and supports effective teaching and learning.

Guidelines for Appropriate Classroom Attire

Choosing appropriate attire as a teacher requires balancing professionalism with approachability, while respecting cultural and institutional norms. Here are key guidelines:

- **Adhere to School Policies**: Follow the school's dress code, which often prohibits casual wear like jeans and t-shirts. This demonstrates respect for school policies and sets a positive example.

- **Prioritize Comfort**: Opt for clothing that allows ease of movement and comfort throughout the day, avoiding restrictive attire or uncomfortable footwear.
- **Reflect Professionalism**: Dress in attire that is professional yet not overly formal. Men may wear collared shirts and trousers, while women can opt for blouses, skirts, or dress pants—ensuring cleanliness, neatness, and appropriateness.
- **Consider Cultural Sensitivities**: Be mindful of cultural norms within the school community when selecting attire. Respectful dressing promotes inclusivity and understanding.
- **Personalize Thoughtfully**: Add personal touches like accessories or colors that reflect personality, maintaining tastefulness and avoiding distractions in the classroom.
- **Maintain Grooming Standards**: Ensure clothes are clean, well-maintained, and presentable. Attention to personal grooming enhances professionalism and serves as a positive example for students.

Key Takeaways

- **Non-Verbal communication shapes classroom dynamics:** Body language, facial expressions, and gestures play a pivotal role in creating a positive and engaging learning environment.
- **Importance of awareness and consistency:** Teachers should be mindful of their non-verbal cues, ensuring they align with their teaching goals and maintain consistency in their expressions.
- **Enhancing teacher-student relationships:** Non-verbal communication builds rapport and trust with students, fostering a supportive and respectful classroom atmosphere.

- **Effective classroom management:** Reading student body language helps in identifying engagement, confusion, and behavioral issues, enabling teachers to respond promptly and effectively.
- **Long-term benefits for teaching effectiveness:** Improving non-verbal communication skills enhances teaching effectiveness, student engagement, and overall educational outcomes.

Chapter 6

The Charismatic Voice

There is no personal charm so great as the charm of a cheerful temperament.

---- Henry Van Dyke

Picture one teacher delivering a lesson in a dull, monotone voice, and another teacher presenting the same lesson with enthusiasm, varying their pitch and pace to emphasize key points. Which teacher do you think would capture students' attention more?

William Arthur Ward, a celebrated educator, famously said, *"The mediocre teacher tells. The good teacher explains. The superior teacher demonstrates. The great teacher inspires."*

This quote underscores the profound effect of vocal delivery in education. Research confirms that vocal cues—**tone, pitch, and pace**—significantly shape students' engagement and perception of lessons.

According to a study by Knapp and Hall (2010), non-verbal communication, including vocal cues, constitutes a substantial part of the communication process, influencing how messages are received and interpreted.

Effective vocal delivery can capture students' attention, convey enthusiasm, and enhance understanding. In this chapter, we will explore the various elements of vocal delivery that contribute to effective teaching.

We will examine techniques for modulating tone, pitch, and pace, and discuss how to use pauses and emphasis to highlight key points. Teachers can create a dynamic and engaging classroom environment that fosters learning and inspiration by mastering these vocal skills.

Fundamentals of Vocal Cues

Vocal cues are the non-verbal elements of speech that include tone, pitch, volume, pace, and pauses. These cues are crucial in communication because they convey emotions, emphasize points, and maintain listener engagement. While words carry the primary message, vocal cues shape how that message is received.

According to Albert Mehrabian's communication model, 38% of meaning is conveyed through vocal elements, highlighting their significant role in effective communication (Mehrabian, 1971).

Understanding Volume, Pace, and Pause

Volume	Pace	Pause
<ul><li>It is the loudness or softness of speech.</li><li>Adjusting volume can emphasize key points, convey excitement or seriousness, and maintain student attention.</li><li>A study by Cleveland (2002) found that varying volume helps keep listeners engaged and underscores the importance of the content being delivered.</li></ul>	<ul><li>It refers to the speed at which someone speaks.</li><li>Speaking too quickly can overwhelm listeners, while a slow pace can bore them. Effective speakers modulate their pace to match the content and the audience's comprehension level.</li><li>Research by Apple et al. (1979) suggests that varying pace helps maintain interest and allows time for information processing.</li></ul>	<ul><li>It is the intentional break in speech.</li><li>Pauses also help speakers gather their thoughts and manage the flow of their presentations.</li><li>According to Beebe and Beebe (2010), strategic pauses enhance the clarity and impact of the message.</li></ul>

In summary, vocal cues like volume, pace, and pauses play a vital role in communication, particularly in educational settings. They help convey emotions, emphasize critical points, and keep the audience engaged. By mastering these elements, you can significantly enhance your classroom presence and effectiveness.

Vocal Mastery: How Martin Luther King Jr. Commanded Attention

There are many leaders whose apt use of their vocal power has made for memorable speeches. One famous example that is on top of my mind is of a speaker who masterfully used his vocal power, Martin Luther King Jr. in his iconic "I Have a Dream" speech. Delivered on August 28, 1963, during the March on Washington for Jobs and Freedom, King's speech is celebrated even today for its profound content and for his powerful vocal delivery.

King's use of volume was particularly impactful. He began his speech in a calm, measured tone, drawing his audience in and creating a sense of intimacy. As he progressed, he strategically increased his volume, particularly when delivering key phrases such as "I have a dream." This escalation in volume emphasized the importance of his vision and helped captivate the audience.

King also varied his pace effectively. He used a slower pace when making crucial points, allowing the audience to fully absorb the weight of his words. For example, when he said, "One hundred years later, the Negro still is not free," the deliberate pace underscored the enduring nature of racial injustice. Conversely, he quickened his pace during more passionate sections, conveying urgency and stirring emotions.

Additionally, King's use of pauses added dramatic effect and gave listeners time to reflect on his powerful statements. His pauses before and after pivotal lines, such as "Free at last, free at last, thank God Almighty, we are free at last," allowed the significance of his message to resonate deeply.

King's adept use of vocal power—through varying volume, pace, and strategic pauses—not only enhanced the emotional impact of his speech but also helped solidify his message in the hearts and minds of his audience, in a way that is relevant even today after decades.

Let's dive into each of the components of vocal power to comprehend the impact that you can make with your vocal cues.

Volume: The Power of Loudness

In the context of vocal delivery, volume refers to the loudness or softness of one's voice. It is a crucial element of communication that can significantly affect how messages are perceived and understood. Volume helps convey **emotions, emphasize points, and engage listeners.** Mastering volume control is essential for teachers to maintain students' attention, ensure clarity, and create an effective learning environment.

Range: The spectrum of volume in vocal delivery ranges from whispering to shouting. Whispering can create intimacy and draw listeners in, often used to convey secrecy or urgency. In contrast, shouting can signal authority, urgency, or strong emotions but must be used sparingly to avoid overwhelming or intimidating the audience. An optimal volume is typically loud enough to be heard clearly but not so loud as to cause discomfort.

Research by Giles and Oxford (1970) suggests that higher volume levels are often associated with confidence and authority, while lower volumes can convey calmness or introspection.

Classroom Application: Teachers can use volume strategically to enhance their delivery. For instance, raising your volume can emphasize critical points, while lowering your volume can create a sense of intimacy and encourage students to listen more closely. Effective volume modulation can also help manage classroom dynamics, such as gaining students' attention or signaling transitions.

The Impact of Volume

Engagement

Varying volume is a powerful tool for capturing and maintaining attention. By modulating loudness, speakers can break the monotony and keep listeners engaged.

Emotion

A louder volume can express enthusiasm, excitement, or urgency, making the content more compelling and impactful. For example, a teacher raising their voice slightly when discussing a significant event in history can heighten the emotional impact, helping students to feel the importance of the moment. On the other hand, softer tones while narrating a sad story can convey empathy, sadness, or seriousness.

Authority

Research by Giles and Oxford (1970) supports this, showing that speakers who use a strong, confident volume are often perceived as more authoritative and credible. However, it's important to balance this with empathy and approachability to avoid coming across as overly aggressive or intimidating.

Putting it into Practice

- **Record and playback:** Record your speech and listen to the playback to become aware of your natural volume range.
- **Diaphragmatic speaking:** Practice speaking from your diaphragm for a fuller, more resonant sound.
- **Breathing exercises:** Use deep diaphragmatic breathing exercises to enhance volume control.
- **Volume variation practice:**
  Read passages aloud, deliberately increasing and decreasing your volume to emphasize key ideas.
- **Decibel monitoring:** Utilize decibel meter apps to monitor and adjust your volume effectively.

Avoiding Pitfalls:

- Monitor Reactions: Pay attention to students' reactions—adjust volume if they seem overwhelmed or are leaning in to hear.
- Avoid Monotony: Vary your volume at regular intervals to maintain interest and emphasize key points.
- Solicit Feedback: Regularly seek feedback from peers or mentors on your volume control.
- Balance Loudness and Softness: Avoid speaking too loudly (aggressive) or too softly (inaudible) for extended periods.

Pace: The Rhythm of Speech

Pace in vocal delivery refers to the speed at which someone speaks. **It encompasses the rate at which words are spoken, the pauses between phrases or sentences, and the overall rhythm of speech.** A well-managed pace can significantly impact how a message is received and understood.

Research indicates that varying the pace of speech can enhance comprehension and listener engagement. For example, a study by McGarrigle and Donaldson (1974) found that moderate variations in speech rate can improve listener attention and comprehension compared to a monotonous rate.

Elements:-

- **Speed:** This refers to how fast or slow one speaks. Speaking too quickly can overwhelm listeners and make it difficult for them to follow along, while speaking too slowly can cause boredom and loss of interest.

- **Rhythm:** This involves the natural flow and variation in speech, including the emphasis on certain words and the use of pauses. A rhythmic pace helps maintain listener interest and aids in comprehension.
- **Pauses:** Strategic pauses can emphasize important points, give listeners time to process information, and make the speaker appear more confident and thoughtful.

In the context of teaching, pacing can significantly impact classroom dynamics.

Teachers who vary their pace appropriately can better hold students' attention, emphasize key points, and maintain a more interactive learning environment.

Educators need to be mindful of their pacing, ensuring it matches the content being taught and the needs of their students.

Understanding and controlling pace is a skill that can be developed through practice and self-awareness. Let us deep dive into the impact of our pace.

The Impact of Pace

Engagement

When a teacher speaks at a steady, moderate pace, it helps students stay focused and attentive.For instance, speeding up the pace slightly when introducing an exciting topic or slowing down during complex explanations can capture and maintain students' attention.

Clarity

Pacing plays a significant role in ensuring that students understand the material being taught. A moderate and consistent pace allows students time to process information and follow along with the lesson. Conversely, speaking too quickly can overwhelm students, leading to confusion and reduced comprehension.

Emotion

By adjusting pacing according to the emotional context of the lesson, teachers can enhance the overall classroom atmosphere and student experience.

Putting it into Practice

- **Metronome exercise:** Use a metronome to set a beat and practice speaking at different speeds. Start with a moderate pace and gradually increase or decrease the speed to find your comfortable speaking rate.

- **Scripted readings:** Choose a passage or text and read it aloud, focusing on maintaining a steady pace. Record yourself and listen back to identify areas where you can adjust your speed.
- **Breath control:** Practice diaphragmatic breathing to support your voice and maintain a steady pace. Breathing exercises can help you control your speed and avoid speaking too quickly.

Avoiding Pitfalls

- Speaking Too Quickly: Rapid speech can overwhelm students and hinder comprehension. Practice slowing down and enunciating clearly.
- Monotonous Pace: A monotone delivery can lead to boredom and disengagement. Vary your pace throughout the lesson to maintain interest.
- Ignoring Student Response: Pay attention to students' non-verbal cues and adjust your pace based on their feedback. Be responsive to their understanding and engagement levels.

Pause: The Power of Silence

A pause in communication refers to a brief period of silence between words or phrases. It serves as a **deliberate break in speech, allowing the speaker and listener time to absorb information and reflect on the message being conveyed.** Pauses are powerful tools that can enhance communication by adding emphasis, clarity, and creating a natural flow in speech.

Types of Pauses

1. **Compositional Pause:** This type of pause occurs naturally in speech patterns, such as between sentences or phrases. It allows the speaker to organize thoughts and provide structure to their speech.
2. **Emphatic Pause:** An emphatic pause is used to draw attention to a specific word or phrase. It adds emphasis and can make the message more impactful. For example, "I want you to know, (pause) you are doing a great job."
3. **Reflective Pause:** This pause allows time for reflection and consideration. It can be used to let the information sink in or to give listeners time to formulate their responses.
4. **Dramatic Pause:** Often used in public speaking and storytelling, a dramatic pause is used for effect. It creates anticipation and can build tension, making the message more memorable.

The Impact of Pause

Emphasis

According to research, pauses have been shown to improve retention and understanding by giving listeners time to process information (Bavelas et al., 1986). For example, in a classroom setting, a teacher might use a pause before stating an important principle or concept, allowing students to mentally prepare to receive the information.

Processing Time

Studies have indicated that pauses in speech allow listeners to mentally organize and store information, which can lead to better comprehension and retention (Fox Tree, 1999). By giving students sufficient time to process information, teachers can facilitate a deeper understanding and application of the content.

Dramatic Effect

Research suggests that well-timed pauses can build suspense and increase engagement by piquing curiosity and creating anticipation (Zuckerman et al., 2014). For instance, a teacher might use a dramatic pause before revealing the outcome of an experiment or the resolution of a problem, thereby heightening interest and involvement among students.

Let us learn how to put it into practice.

Putting it into Practice

- **Practice timing:** Experiment with different lengths of pauses—short, medium, and long—to see what feels natural and impactful.
- **Breath awareness:** Become aware of your breathing patterns. Use breaths to naturally punctuate your speech with pauses.
- **Use of silence:** Embrace silence intentionally. Allow it to naturally occur when you finish a sentence or make a critical point.

- **Listen to recordings:** Record yourself teaching and listen back to identify where you can insert effective pauses.
- **Practice with scripts:** Use scripts or outlines to plan where to pause for emphasis.

Avoiding Pitfalls

- Overuse: Avoid using too many pauses, as this can disrupt the flow of your teaching.
- Inconsistent Pauses: Ensure your pauses are consistent in length and frequency to maintain a natural rhythm.
- Nervous Pausing: Avoid using pauses to fill gaps when you are nervous or unsure.
- Misplaced Pauses: Be mindful of where you place pauses in sentences to avoid confusion or misinterpretation.
- Not Pausing for Response: After asking a question, ensure you give students adequate time to respond before moving on.

Integrating volume, pace, and pause in vocal delivery is crucial for creating a dynamic and engaging classroom environment. These elements work synergistically to emphasize key points, maintain attention, and convey emotions effectively.

I highly encourage all teachers to focus on improving their vocal cues as in the journey of education, the voice of a teacher is not just a means of conveying knowledge; it is a powerful instrument for inspiring, motivating, and shaping the minds of future generations.

Reflect on Your Vocal Mastery

Take a quiz and reflect on the elements we learned today. Check the boxes with the score you want to give yourself, **1** being for the area that needs **significant improvement**, **2** being for the part where you are **good but there is room for a little improvement,** and **3** for the part which you believe you have **mastered**.

Criteria	Rating		
	1	**2**	**3**
I use a dramatic pause while telling a story.			
I vary my volume to emphasize key points.			
I maintain an engaging pace that keeps listeners' interest.			
I project my voice clearly so everyone can hear.			
I adjust my tone to convey different emotions.			
I avoid monotone speech to keep my audience engaged.			
I use vocal variety to maintain interest.			

I use emphasis on important words or phrases.			
I ensure my speech is clear and articulate.			

Give yourself a pat on the back for the areas in which you scored 3, **flash a big smile** where you scored 2 as you are doing good and you can further improve. **Closely analyze** the areas where you scored 1.

Key Takeaways

- **Vocal cues enhance communication**: Mastering vocal elements such as volume, pace, and pause can significantly enhance communication in the classroom. Varying these cues can capture students' attention and improve comprehension.

- **Impact on engagement and understanding**: Adjusting volume, pace, and pause can keep students engaged, aid in information processing, and emphasize key points. This contributes to a more effective learning environment.

- **Building connection and authority**: Using vocal cues to convey warmth and confidence helps in building a positive rapport with students. It establishes authority and boosts teacher-student relationships.

- **Practical application is key**: Practical exercises to practice volume control, pacing, and strategic pausing are essential for teachers to integrate these techniques effectively into their teaching style.

- **Continuous improvement**: Encouraging teachers to focus on improving their vocal delivery is crucial. It can enhance their teaching effectiveness, student engagement, and overall classroom dynamics.

Chapter 7

Charisma In Classroom: Engaging Students

True Charisma comes from a genuine desire to understand and uplift others.

---Michelle Obama

Imagine entering a classroom where the students are eagerly leaning forward, eyes sparkling with interest as the teacher speaks. This teacher isn't just delivering a lesson; they're weaving a captivating story, peppered with humor that makes even the most complex concepts memorable. This is the power of charisma in teaching, embodied by teachers who leave a lasting impression on their students.

Profile of a Charismatic Teacher

Those of us lucky enough to have been students of charismatic teachers know their exceptional ability to captivate our attention not only for an entire class period but also throughout the course or school year. Their classrooms have an electric quality that leaves a lasting impression, fondly remembered and greatly admired, yet rarely replicated by other teachers with equal knowledge and experience.

To nurture the development of qualities inherent to truly inspiring teaching, it's crucial to first identify these qualities. Drawing from Milojkovic and Zimbardo's (1980) insights and my own classroom experiences as a student of electrifying masters, I've outlined a profile of the quintessential charismatic teacher. Here are the key attributes:

- **Total Mastery:** Charismatic teachers strive to be the absolute master of their domain, ensuring every concept they present is fully thought through.

- **Joy in the Quest for Understanding:** A charismatic teacher's delight in their field is evident and contagious. Through self-disclosures, they share the sophisticated thought processes that have led to their current understanding.

- **Insatiable Curiosity:** They are never delighted with their current level of understanding and continually seek deeper explanations, learning from every teaching encounter and being open to new ideas.

- **Sincerity:** They genuinely believe in the importance of their field and are committed to furthering it.

- **Flawless Presentation:** They aim for a smooth and precise delivery, where technical details are seamlessly integrated, making their teaching flow effortlessly.

- **Overt Assertiveness:** They present my interpretations and analyses with vigor, convinced of their internal consistency and completeness, projecting an infectious confidence.

- **High Energy Level:** They approach everything with dynamic force and full-hearted enthusiasm.

- **Dramatic Appreciation:** They combine a sense of the dramatic with an acute appreciation of timing to enhance my teaching.

- **Clear Affect:** They express their emotional reactions clearly through their facial expressions, body movements, and tone of voice.

- **Positive Self-Image:** They maintain a positive self-regard, conveying no doubts about their self-worth.

- **Sense of Perspective:** Their clear perception of the context of their discipline highlights the importance of outstanding problems in the field.
- **Unity of Purpose:** They guide their students toward a shared goal – the enrichment of both intellect and spirit.

By embodying these qualities, let's aim to create an engaging and inspiring classroom atmosphere that fosters deep learning and lasting impact.

Charisma in teaching goes beyond delivering the content of books; it transforms the learning experience. Charismatic teachers captivate their students' attention, foster a positive learning environment, and enhance student engagement and retention.

Their ability to connect with students personally, combined with their dynamic presentation skills, makes learning both enjoyable and effective.

Charisma and its Impact on Students

The presence of a charismatic teacher can significantly influence student engagement, motivation, and learning outcomes. When students are engaged, they are more likely to participate actively in class, ask questions, and seek further knowledge. A charismatic teacher's enthusiasm is contagious; it motivates students to take an interest in the subject matter and strive for academic excellence. For instance, when a teacher passionately explains a complex scientific concept, students are more likely to find it intriguing and worth understanding.

Moreover, charismatic teachers often establish a strong rapport with their students, creating a supportive and trusting classroom atmosphere. This rapport can boost students' self-esteem and confidence, encouraging them to take risks and explore new ideas. Such teachers also use their charisma to manage classroom behavior effectively, reducing disruptions and maintaining a focus on learning.

Several studies have highlighted the effectiveness of charismatic teaching. Research indicates that students taught by charismatic teachers show higher levels of academic achievement and improved attitudes toward learning.

For example, a study published in the **Journal of Educational Psychology** found that students perceived charismatic teachers as more competent and credible, which in turn enhanced their motivation and learning outcomes.

Another study by the **University of Warwick** revealed that charismatic teaching positively impacts students' emotional and cognitive engagement. This study emphasized that charismatic teachers often use expressive **body** language, varied vocal tones, and dynamic gestures to maintain students' attention and interest. Additionally, these teachers frequently incorporate storytelling and humor into their lessons, making the material more relatable and easier to remember.

Charisma in teaching also correlates with increased student attendance and reduced dropout rates. Students are more likely to attend classes regularly when they look forward to the engaging and dynamic instruction of a charismatic teacher. Furthermore, the positive relationships formed between charismatic teachers and their students can provide the emotional support necessary to persevere through academic challenges.

Charisma in teaching is not merely about being likable or entertaining; it is about creating an environment that fosters engagement, motivation, and effective learning. Charismatic teachers inspire students to become active participants in their education, leading to improved academic outcomes and a more enjoyable learning experience. Let's explore three ways to enhance your charisma in the classroom.

#1 Power of Humour

Humor in education involves the use of amusing anecdotes, jokes, and playful interactions to create a more engaging and enjoyable learning environment. When effectively integrated into teaching, humor can break the monotony of routine lectures, capture students' attention, and make the learning process more dynamic. It helps build a positive classroom atmosphere, fosters stronger relationships between teachers and students, and can even make the most boring, complex, or dry subject matter more accessible and memorable for your students.

Benefits of Using Humor in Teaching

1. Reducing Anxiety

One of the primary benefits of incorporating humor into teaching is its ability to reduce anxiety and stress among students. Classrooms can often be high-pressure environments where students feel the weight of academic expectations and social dynamics. Humor can act as a natural stress reliever, providing a momentary escape from these pressures.

For instance, I try to lighten the mood of my students with a funny story at the beginning of a test. This helps to ease students' nerves, enabling them to perform better.

According to research published in the **Journal of Educational Psychology,** students in classrooms where teachers use humor report lower levels of anxiety and a greater sense of comfort.

2. Increasing Retention and Understanding

Humor can also enhance the retention and comprehension of information. When students find something funny, they are more likely to pay attention and remember it. This is because humor often involves surprising or novel elements that capture attention and stimulate cognitive processes. For example, a teacher might use a humorous analogy to explain a complex scientific concept, making it easier for students to understand and recall the information later. A study by Kaplan and Pascoe (1977) found that humor in teaching significantly improved students' retention of lecture material, demonstrating its effectiveness as a pedagogical tool.

3. Fostering a Positive Classroom Environment

Using humor can help create a warm and inclusive classroom environment where students feel more comfortable participating. Laughter and shared jokes can break down barriers between the teacher and students, promoting a sense of community and trust. This positive atmosphere encourages students to engage more freely, ask questions, and express their ideas without fear of judgment. For instance, a teacher who occasionally uses self-deprecating humor can show students that it's okay to make mistakes and that learning is a process.

4. Enhancing Student-Teacher Relationships

Humor can strengthen the bond between teachers and students by humanizing the teacher and making them more approachable.

When teachers use humor appropriately, it shows students that they are relatable and empathetic, which can lead to better communication and understanding. A teacher who shares a funny personal story or jokes about everyday classroom occurrences can build rapport and create a more collaborative and respectful classroom dynamic.

5. Encouraging Creative Thinking

Humor often involves thinking outside the box and seeing situations from different perspectives, which can stimulate students' creative thinking skills. When teachers use humorous examples or encourage students to come up with their own funny analogies or scenarios, it can promote divergent thinking and problem-solving abilities.

For example, in a literature class, a teacher might ask students to rewrite a serious scene from a novel in a humorous style, encouraging them to engage with the material in a novel way.

Types of Humor in the Classroom

1. Spontaneous Humor

Spontaneous humor refers to unplanned, in-the-moment jokes or funny remarks that arise naturally during a lesson. This type of humor can be particularly effective in capturing students' attention and making the classroom atmosphere more relaxed and engaging. For example, if a student gives an unexpected answer or if something amusing happens during a lesson, a teacher can make a quick, light-hearted comment to capitalize on the moment. Spontaneous humor shows students that the teacher is attentive and can think on their feet, fostering a dynamic and interactive learning environment. However, it's important for teachers to be mindful of their audience and ensure that spontaneous jokes are always appropriate and inclusive.

2. Planned Humor

Planned humor involves preparing jokes, funny anecdotes, or humorous examples in advance that are relevant to the lesson content. This type of humor can be woven into the teaching material to make it more interesting and memorable. For instance, a history teacher might tell a humorous story about a historical figure or event to illustrate a point, or a math teacher could use a funny cartoon to explain a complex concept. Planned humor allows teachers to thoughtfully integrate humor into their lessons in a way that supports and enhances the learning objectives. By preparing in advance, teachers can ensure that the humor is appropriate and aligns with the educational goals of the lesson.

3. Self-Deprecating Humor

Self-deprecating humor involves making jokes at one's own expense. This type of humor can be very effective in building rapport with students, as it shows humility and relatability. When teachers laugh at their own mistakes or quirks, it humanizes them and makes them more approachable. For example, a teacher might joke about their own difficulties with a subject when they were a student, making students feel more comfortable with their own struggles. Self-deprecating humor can break down barriers and create a more relaxed and open classroom atmosphere. However, it's important for teachers to use this type of humor sparingly and ensure it doesn't undermine their authority or professionalism.

Case Study 1: A Teacher Effectively Using Humor to Explain a Complex Concept

Mrs. Jones, a high school chemistry teacher, faced the daunting task of teaching her students the periodic table. Recognizing the potential for dry, rote learning, she decided to infuse humor into her lessons. Instead of merely listing elements, she created funny, memorable stories for each one. For example, she described helium as "the party animal of the elements, always floating around at high altitudes and making voices squeaky." This playful approach not only made the content more engaging but also helped students remember the characteristics and uses of different elements. Mrs. Jones' students reported higher levels of interest and retention, demonstrating how humor can make complex subjects more approachable and enjoyable.

Case Study 2: The Impact of Humor on a Particularly Challenging Class

Mr. Smith taught a middle school math class notorious for its disruptive behavior and lack of engagement. Determined to turn the tide, he incorporated humor into his lessons. He started each class with a math-related joke or a humorous math problem. One day, he asked, "Why was the equal sign so humble?" and answered, "Because it knew it wasn't less than or greater than anyone else." The students began to look forward to his classes, and the humor helped to create a more relaxed and positive atmosphere. Over time, Mr. Smith noticed a significant improvement in behavior and participation. Students were more willing to tackle difficult problems, and the overall class dynamic became more cooperative and supportive. This case highlights the transformative power of humor in managing classroom challenges and fostering a positive learning environment.

Putting It into Practice

- **Know your audience**: Tailor your humor to the age, interests, and cultural backgrounds of your students. What works for high school students might not be appropriate for younger children, and cultural sensitivity is crucial to ensure inclusivity and respect.
- **Timing and delivery**: Introduce humor at moments that can enhance the lesson or relieve tension, such as after explaining a complex concept or during a transition between activities. Ensure your delivery is confident and natural; forced humor can fall flat.
- **Keep it relevant**: Use humor that directly relates to the lesson content. This not only makes the humor more effective but also reinforces the material being taught. For example, a science joke can make a complex concept more memorable.
- **Avoiding pitfalls**: Steer clear of sarcasm, which can be easily misunderstood and hurtful. Avoid jokes that could be offensive, inappropriate, or marginalizing. Ensure your humor is positive, inclusive, and enhances the classroom environment without alienating or offending any student.

#2 Power of Story-telling

Storytelling has long been a cornerstone of human communication and education. Stories resonate with people on a deep level, tapping into our natural inclination to connect with narratives. They can simplify complex information, making it more accessible and engaging for students. Unlike traditional lecture methods that may fail to capture students' interest, stories provide context and relevance, helping students see the practical application of what they are learning.

They introduce elements of suspense, conflict, and resolution that keep listeners hooked. This engagement is crucial in a classroom setting where maintaining students' attention can be challenging. Stories resonate with people on a deep level, tapping into our natural inclination to connect with narratives. They can simplify complex information, making it more accessible and engaging for students. Unlike traditional lecture methods that may fail to capture students' interest, stories provide context and relevance, helping students see the practical application of what they are learning.

Moreover, stories are inherently engaging. They introduce elements of suspense, conflict, and resolution that keep listeners hooked. This engagement is crucial in a classroom setting where maintaining students' attention can be challenging. When students are engaged, they are more likely to participate actively, ask questions, and engage in discussions, which enhances their learning experience.

Stories captivate our attention, evoke emotions, and make complex ideas more relatable. In the classroom, storytelling is a powerful teaching tool that can transform abstract concepts into memorable narratives.

Benefits of Storytelling for Memory Retention and Engagement

1. **Memory Retention**: One of the significant benefits of storytelling in education is its impact on memory retention. According to cognitive psychologists, stories are easier to remember than isolated facts or figures. This is because stories create a mental framework that helps students organize and recall information more efficiently. When students hear a story, they can link new knowledge to the narrative, making it easier to retrieve later. Research by psychologist Jerome Bruner suggests that people are 22 times more likely to remember information when it is presented as a story compared to a list of facts.

2. **Emotional Connection**: Stories evoke emotions, which play a critical role in memory formation and retention. When students feel emotionally connected to a story, the information it conveys becomes more meaningful and memorable. This emotional engagement can also foster a deeper understanding of the material, as students relate the content to their own experiences and emotions.

3. **Enhancing Engagement**: Storytelling naturally captures students' attention and keeps them engaged. A well-told story can turn a mundane lesson into an exciting and immersive experience. This engagement is particularly beneficial in subjects that students might find challenging or uninteresting. For instance, a history lesson about ancient civilizations can become more vivid and compelling when framed as a narrative about the daily lives, struggles, and triumphs of people from that era.

4. **Developing Critical Thinking Skills**: Stories often involve characters facing dilemmas, making decisions, and experiencing consequences. Discussing these elements in the classroom encourages students to think critically and analyze situations from

different perspectives. This analytical thinking can be applied across various subjects, helping students develop a more nuanced understanding of the material.

5. **Promoting Empathy and Cultural Awareness**: Through stories, students can explore diverse cultures, historical periods, and viewpoints. This exposure fosters empathy and cultural awareness, encouraging students to appreciate and respect differences. It also helps them understand the broader context of the content they are learning, making it more relevant and meaningful.

6. **Facilitating Discussion and Collaboration**: Storytelling can serve as a springboard for class discussions and collaborative activities. After hearing a story, students can be prompted to share their interpretations, ask questions, and work together to explore the themes and lessons within the narrative. This collaborative learning environment can enhance students' communication and teamwork skills.

Storytelling is a potent educational tool that enhances memory retention, engagement, critical thinking, and empathy.

By integrating storytelling into your teaching methods, you can create a more dynamic and effective learning experience for your students.

Elements of Effective Storytelling

1. Structure

An effective story follows a clear structure, typically comprising a beginning, middle, and end. This structure helps in organizing the narrative and guiding the audience through the story in a coherent manner. The beginning sets the stage by introducing the characters, setting, and initial situation. It provides the necessary background information that allows students to understand the context of the story.

The middle is where the plot develops, presenting challenges and conflicts that the characters must navigate. This section maintains students' interest by creating tension and suspense. The end brings the story to a resolution, where conflicts are resolved, and the narrative reaches a satisfying conclusion. This structure not only helps in maintaining engagement but also ensures that the educational objectives of the story are clearly communicated.

2. Characters

Characters are the heart of any story. To be effective in a classroom setting, characters should be relatable and memorable. Relatable characters help students see aspects of themselves or people they know, which makes the story more impactful. They don't need to be perfect; in fact, flaws and challenges make characters more human and engaging. Memorable characters are those that stand out due to their distinct personalities, goals, and behaviors. When students can connect with characters on a personal level, they become more invested in the narrative and its outcomes. For instance, in a science lesson, a character who struggles with and eventually overcomes a difficult experiment can inspire students to persevere in their own studies.

3. Conflict and Resolution

Conflict is essential in storytelling as it introduces tension and challenges that need to be overcome. This element keeps students engaged by providing a sense of anticipation and curiosity about how the characters will resolve their issues. The conflict can be external, such as a character facing an obstacle or antagonist, or internal, involving personal struggles and growth.

Resolution is equally important as it provides closure to the story, addressing the conflict and delivering the key messages or lessons. In educational storytelling, the resolution often reinforces the learning objectives, ensuring that students walk away with a clear understanding of the lesson. For example, in a history lesson about civil rights, the conflict might involve characters fighting for equality, with the resolution highlighting the importance of perseverance and justice.

Putting it into Practice

- **Personal stories:** Sharing personal anecdotes is a powerful way to build connections with students. When teachers share their own experiences, it humanizes them and makes the lesson more relatable. For instance, a math teacher might share a story about struggling with a math problem as a child and how they overcame it, which can inspire students to persist through their own challenges.
- **Relating to curriculum:** Integrating stories with lesson objectives helps reinforce learning. For example, a history teacher

might use a narrative about a historical figure to explain broader historical events. This not only makes the content more engaging but also aids in memory retention by providing a narrative framework for the facts.

- **Use of voice and body language:** Enhancing the story with vocal variety and gestures can make it more compelling. Changing the pitch, pace, and volume of your voice helps emphasize key points and keeps students interested. Similarly, using gestures and body movements can help illustrate parts of the story, making it more dynamic and memorable.

- **Visual aids and props:** Incorporating visuals such as pictures, videos, and props can make stories more vivid. For example, in a science lesson, a teacher could use models or diagrams to demonstrate a scientific concept being narrated. Visual aids not only capture students' attention but also help in concretizing abstract ideas, making them easier to understand and remember.

Charisma Hacks to Blend Humor and Storytelling in Lessons

1. **Relevance and Context**: Ensure that humor and storytelling align with the lesson objectives and content. Humor should complement the narrative rather than distract from it.

2. **Natural Flow**: Introduce humor and storytelling at appropriate moments to maintain the flow of the lesson. For instance, use humor to lighten the mood after explaining a complex concept or to segue into a new topic.

3. **Character Development**: Use storytelling to create relatable characters or scenarios that resonate with students. Inject humor through these characters' interactions or dilemmas.

4. **Pacing and Timing**: Practice timing to deliver punchlines effectively within the narrative structure. Pause for laughter or reflection where appropriate to enhance impact.

Examples of Lessons that Effectively Integrate Both Techniques:

- **Science Class**: Introduce a humorous anecdote about a historical scientific discovery before delving into the scientific principles behind it.
- **Literature Class**: Use storytelling to bring characters from a novel to life, incorporating humor through their dialogues or actions.

Overcoming Challenges

A. Addressing Resistance: Not all students may find humor or storytelling engaging. To handle this:

- **Alternative Approaches**: Use humor and storytelling as part of a diverse teaching toolkit, adapting to various learning preferences.
- **Individualization**: Understand students' interests and tailor humor and stories to fit their personalities and learning styles.
- **Respect Preferences**: Adjust your approach if a student shows discomfort or disinterest to maintain inclusivity and engagement.

B. Cultural Sensitivity: In a culturally diverse classroom, sensitivity is crucial for effective teaching:

- **Awareness and Education**: Educate yourself about the cultural backgrounds and norms of your students. Avoid stereotypes and ensure that your humor and stories are respectful and inclusive of all cultural identities.

- **Adaptation**: Modify your stories and humor to be culturally relevant and appropriate. Incorporate examples and perspectives that reflect the diversity of your students.
- **Open Dialogue**: Foster an environment where students feel comfortable discussing cultural differences. Encourage respectful dialogue and mutual understanding among students from different backgrounds.

By addressing resistance with alternative approaches and promoting cultural sensitivity, teachers can create an inclusive and engaging classroom environment where humor and storytelling can effectively enhance learning experiences for all students.

#3 Power of Dressing Well

As a teacher, I have come to understand that my appearance plays a significant role in my charisma and the overall classroom environment. The way I present myself not only affects how my students perceive me but also influences my own confidence and effectiveness as an educator. Here are some key points on how my appearance impacts my charisma in the classroom:

- **Professionalism:** I ensure my attire reflects professionalism, which sets the tone for the classroom and establishes my authority from the start.
- **Approachability:** By dressing in a way that is both professional and approachable, I make myself more accessible to my students, encouraging open communication.
- **Confidence:** When I dress well, I feel more confident, and this confidence is conveyed through my body language and interactions, enhancing my overall charisma.

- **Respect:** A well-groomed appearance earns me respect from my students and colleagues, reinforcing my position and making it easier to maintain classroom discipline.

- **Consistency:** I maintain a consistent and reliable appearance, which helps build trust with my students as they perceive me as dependable and serious about my role.

- **Attention to Detail:** My attention to detail in my appearance demonstrates to my students that I value and respect the learning environment, encouraging them to do the same.

- **Cultural Sensitivity:** By being mindful of cultural and institutional dress codes, I show respect for the diverse backgrounds of my students, fostering a more inclusive classroom.

- **Non-Verbal Communication:** My appearance is a powerful non-verbal cue that communicates my readiness, enthusiasm, and commitment to teaching, which positively influences my students' engagement and perception of me.

- **First Impressions:** I understand that first impressions are lasting, so I make sure my appearance on the first day sets a positive, lasting tone for the rest of the term.

- **Role Modeling:** By dressing appropriately, I model the behavior I expect from my students, teaching them the importance of presenting themselves well in professional settings.

Key Takeaways

- **Connection through humor:** Humor fosters rapport and breaks down barriers between teachers and students, creating a more inclusive and enjoyable learning environment.

- **Memorable learning:** Storytelling makes lessons more engaging and memorable by framing concepts within narrative contexts that students can relate to and remember.

- **Effective communication:** Both humor and storytelling enhance communication effectiveness, helping teachers convey complex ideas in accessible ways.

- **Versatility and adaptability:** Teachers should experiment with different types of humor and storytelling styles to find what resonates best with their students, adapting their approach based on feedback and outcomes.

- **Continuous improvement:** Embracing continuous learning and professional development in humor and storytelling techniques allows teachers to evolve and refine their charismatic teaching skills over time, maximizing student engagement and learning outcomes.

- **Your appearance:** A teacher's appearance significantly influences their charisma and the overall classroom atmosphere, affecting both student perception and teacher confidence.

Chapter 8

Commanding The Meeting Room

Charisma is not about being the center of attention; it's about making others feel seen and valued.

---- **Oprah Winfrey**

In the school where I once worked, I had the opportunity to lead the primary section as a Head of Section, marking a significant advancement in my career. A regular event that both intrigued and challenged me was the **Monday morning huddle** in the boardroom. During these sessions, each section head, including myself, was tasked with presenting a report on the previous week—highlighting successes and addressing challenges.

Despite feeling confident in my role, I often found myself dreading these meetings. It wasn't a lack of confidence but rather a sense that I wasn't effectively capturing attention or building trust during these crucial sessions. The format typically involved starting with the challenges and problems encountered. All the teachers in the meeting room including me used the same approach.

One Monday, I decided to take a different approach. Instead of diving straight into the issues, I framed my report as a story. "Last week was filled with highs and lows, much like any other week," I began. I recounted an incident where an upset parent approached me about their child's needs being overlooked. Rather than dwelling on the problem, I described how I facilitated a meeting between the parent and the teacher involved. Together, we resolved the issue, ensuring the child's needs were met, and the parent left the school campus with a smile on their face.

This **storytelling approach** was met with unexpected positive reactions from my colleagues and the principal. It was clear they appreciated the constructive and solution-oriented narrative amidst the usual litany of challenges. This experience taught me a valuable lesson: **the power of storytelling and anecdotes in capturing attention, conveying leadership, and fostering trust in boardroom settings.**

From that day forward, I made it a point to lead with positives and frame challenges as opportunities for growth and improvement. This shift not only enhanced my presence in boardroom meetings but also strengthened my ability to influence and lead effectively within the school community.

In this chapter, we will delve into the process of being a charismatic voice in a meeting room.

Impact:

Charisma plays a crucial role in enhancing leadership, decision-making, and team dynamics within a meeting room. A charismatic teacher or educational leader can:

- **Inspire and Motivate:** Charismatic leaders energize their team, fostering a positive and motivated work environment. Their enthusiasm is contagious, encouraging others to strive for excellence.

- **Facilitate Decision-Making:** Through clear and compelling communication, charismatic leaders can present ideas persuasively, making it easier to reach a consensus and make informed decisions.

- **Build Trust and Credibility:** Charismatic individuals often exude confidence and sincerity, which helps in building trust and credibility among team members and stakeholders. This trust is essential for effective collaboration and implementation of policies.

- **Enhance Team Dynamics:** By fostering a sense of unity and purpose, charismatic leaders can improve team dynamics, ensuring that everyone works towards common goals with a shared vision.

Difference Between Classroom and Meeting Room Charisma:

Classroom Charisma	Meeting Room Charisma
In the classroom, charisma is often about engaging students, making lessons interesting, and fostering a love for learning. It involves a lot of energy, storytelling, and interactive teaching methods.	In the boardroom, charisma focuses more on leadership and influence. It involves presenting ideas clearly, persuading stakeholders, and facilitating discussions to drive strategic decisions. The energy is more controlled and directed towards achieving specific outcomes.

Do's and Don'ts in a Meeting

Aspects	Do's	Don'ts
Body Language	Maintain eye contact to show engagement.	Avoid crossing arms, which can seem defensive.
	Use open gestures to convey openness and confidence.	Fidgeting, tapping, or excessive movements can be distracting.
	Mirror the body language of others to build rapport.	Avoid looking at your phone or watch, which signals disinterest.
Posture	Sit up straight to convey confidence and attentiveness.	Slouching can signal disinterest or lack of energy.
	Lean slightly forward to show interest in the discussion.	Leaning back too much can appear too relaxed or disengaged.
Verbal Cues	Speak clearly and at a moderate pace.	Avoid mumbling or speaking too quickly.
	Use varied intonation to keep the audience engaged.	Monotone speech can be boring and disengaging.
	Be concise and to the point.	Over-explaining or rambling can lose the audience's

		attention.
Facial Expressions	Smile genuinely to convey warmth and approachability.	Avoid excessive facial expressions that can be distracting.
	Use expressions that match the tone of your message.	Avoid neutral or blank expressions that may appear disinterested.
Hand Gestures	Use hand gestures to emphasize points and convey enthusiasm.	Avoid overusing gestures, which can be distracting.
	Keep gestures within the frame of your body for a professional look.	Pointing fingers can seem aggressive.
Listening	Nod occasionally to show understanding and agreement.	Interrupting others can seem disrespectful.
	Take notes to show you value others' input.	Avoid looking bored or distracted when others are speaking.
Engagement	Ask questions to show	Dominating the conversation

	interest and clarify points	can alienate others.
	Paraphrase what others say to show you're listening.	Avoid dismissive or sarcastic remarks.
Attire	Dress appropriately for the meeting's context.	Avoid overly casual or inappropriate attire
	Ensure your attire is neat and professional.	Wearing distracting accessories can draw attention away from your message.
Preparation	Prepare thoroughly and be ready to contribute	Avoid coming unprepared, which can signal lack of interest or competence.
	Bring all necessary materials and documents.	Forgetting essential materials can be seen as unprofessional.

Recipe for Effective Speaking

Integrating anecdotes, questions, active listening, and structured speaking can synergistically enhance communication effectiveness and charisma in boardroom settings. Here's how these elements work together and practical exercises to reinforce their integration:

Synergy of Elements:

1. **Anecdotes:** Anecdotes add a personal touch and make abstract ideas relatable, capturing attention and fostering emotional connection with the audience.
2. **Questions:** Well-crafted questions demonstrate engagement and curiosity, encouraging dialogue, deeper exploration of ideas, and critical thinking among team members.
3. **Active Listening:** Actively listening demonstrates respect and empathy, ensuring that ideas are understood and acknowledged, thus building trust and rapport.
4. **Structured Speaking:** A clear structure enhances clarity and persuasiveness, guiding the audience through key points and ensuring coherence in the presentation.

We will discuss each of these components moving forward in this chapter.

Why Anecdotes Work

Anecdotes, or brief, illustrative stories, are powerful tools in communication due to their psychological and emotional impact on listeners. They work on multiple levels to make messages more compelling and memorable.

Human brains are wired to process and retain stories better than abstract information.

This is because stories activate multiple areas of the brain, including those responsible for sensory experiences, emotions, and motor responses. When listeners hear a story, they visualize the events, empathize with the characters, and emotionally engage with the outcome. This multisensory engagement leads to better retention and understanding.

Anecdotes have the power to evoke **emotions**, which can significantly enhance persuasiveness. Emotions play a crucial role in decision-making, as they influence how information is perceived and processed. When a speaker shares a personal or relatable story, it can elicit feelings such as empathy, joy, sadness, or excitement in the audience. These emotional responses create a bond between the speaker and the listeners, making the message more impactful and memorable.

Abstract concepts can be challenging to grasp without concrete examples. Anecdotes provide specific instances that illustrate these ideas, making them more relatable and understandable.

For instance, explaining the importance of resilience in educational leadership can be abstract, but sharing a story about a principal who overcame significant challenges to improve their school makes the concept tangible and real.

Anecdotes help listeners put themselves in the shoes of others, **fostering empathy** and a deeper understanding of different perspectives. When educational leaders share stories about their experiences or those of others, they humanize their messages, making them more relatable and impactful. This empathetic connection is crucial for building trust and rapport with colleagues, students, and stakeholders.

Anecdotes are also powerful **persuasion** tools. They can highlight the benefits of a particular approach, demonstrate the consequences of certain actions, and provide evidence for arguments. For example, a teacher advocating for a new teaching method might share a success story from their classroom, showing how the method improved student engagement and learning outcomes. This real-life example can be more persuasive than statistics or theoretical arguments alone.

How To Craft Effective Anecdotes

There are three things that you should understand to craft compelling anecdotes.

Relevance: Choosing anecdotes relevant to the topic at hand is essential for engaging the audience and reinforcing the message. Research indicates that stories can enhance learning and retention by making abstract concepts concrete and relatable. A well-chosen anecdote that aligns with the topic helps listeners connect the narrative to the broader context. **For example, if discussing the importance of resilience in leadership, sharing a story about overcoming obstacles in an educational setting can vividly illustrate the concept, making it more impactful and memorable.**

Structure: Anecdotes should follow a clear structure with a beginning, middle, and end. This structure ensures the narrative is coherent and easy to follow. According to cognitive psychology, structured stories are easier for the brain to process and remember. The beginning sets the scene, providing necessary context and background information. The middle presents the main events or challenges, building suspense and highlighting key moments. The end offers a resolution, demonstrating the outcome and its relevance to the topic. **For instance, starting with the description of a challenging school environment, moving through the strategies employed to overcome these challenges, and concluding with the positive outcomes achieved can effectively convey the message.**

Emotional Appeal: Incorporating elements that evoke emotion is crucial for making anecdotes engaging and memorable.

Emotions play a significant role in how we process and remember information. **Neuroscientific research has shown that emotional arousal can enhance memory consolidation.** To evoke emotion, include vivid descriptions, personal reflections, and relatable experiences. Describing the emotional struggles and triumphs of individuals involved in the story can create an emotional connection with the audience. Highlighting moments of joy, frustration, or relief can evoke empathy and make the story more compelling. An emotionally charged anecdote can leave a lasting impression, motivating the audience to reflect on the message and apply it to their own experiences.

By ensuring relevance, maintaining a clear structure, and incorporating emotional appeal, anecdotes can become powerful tools for effective communication, particularly in educational leadership, where storytelling can inspire and influence both colleagues and students.

Putting it into Practice

- **Identify the message:** Determine the core message you want to convey. Ensure the anecdote aligns with this message to reinforce your point.
- **Choose a relevant story:** Select a story that is directly related to the topic at hand. Personal experiences or real-life examples from the school environment are often the most impactful.

- **Structure the anecdote:**
  - Beginning: Set the scene and introduce the main characters or context.
  - Middle: Describe the challenges or pivotal moments, building suspense or interest.
  - End: Conclude with the resolution and highlight how it relates to the message.
- **Add emotional appeal:** Include details that evoke emotions, such as personal reflections or vivid descriptions of the events.
- **Practice delivery:** Rehearse your anecdote to ensure a smooth, confident delivery. Pay attention to your tone, pace, and body language to enhance the story's impact.

Ask Questions

Imagine walking into a boardroom where the CEO of a leading tech company, known for her sharp intellect and decisive leadership, is conducting a critical meeting. The room is filled with senior executives and department heads, all eagerly waiting to discuss the company's next big project.

As the meeting progresses, the CEO doesn't just dictate the agenda or deliver monologues; she strategically asks questions that drive the conversation forward, spark innovation, and foster engagement among the participants.Asking questions is a powerful tool for educational leaders in the boardroom. It demonstrates leadership by showing that you value input, encourage participation, and foster a culture of curiosity and collaboration.

Research supports the effectiveness of asking questions. According to a study published in the Harvard Business Review, leaders who ask questions are perceived as more competent and likable. This perception can enhance their ability to influence and guide their teams effectively. Additionally, asking questions can stimulate critical thinking and problem-solving, essential skills in any educational setting.

When you ask questions, it signals your openness to diverse perspectives and a willingness to engage in meaningful dialogue. This can lead to more innovative solutions and a stronger sense of shared purpose among team members.

Types of Questions

1. **Open-ended Questions**: Open-ended questions are designed to encourage discussion and deeper thinking. They cannot be answered with a simple "yes" or "no" and require thoughtful responses.

Examples include:

"What are your thoughts on the new curriculum changes?" **or** *"How do you feel about the current student engagement strategies?"*

2. **Closed-ended Questions:** Closed-ended questions are used to gather specific information quickly. They can be answered with a "yes," "no," or a specific piece of data.

Examples include:

"Did the test scores improve after implementing the new teaching method?" **or** *"How many students participated in the after-school program last semester?"*

However, overuse of closed-ended questions can stifle conversation, so they should be balanced with open-ended inquiries.

3. **Probing Questions:** Probing questions delve deeper into subjects and uncover underlying issues. They are follow-up questions that prompt respondents to expand on their initial answers.

Examples include:

"Can you explain more about the challenges you faced with the new curriculum?" **or** *"What do you think are the root causes of the decline in student participation?"*

4. **Reflective Questions:** Reflective questions encourage self-reflection and deeper understanding. They prompt individuals to consider their own experiences and insights. Examples include: *"How has your teaching style evolved over the past year?"* **or** *"What have you learned from the recent changes in our educational policies?"*

A study by the University of California, Berkeley, found that leaders who ask questions facilitate better team communication and collaboration, leading to more effective decision-making. By using a mix of open-ended, closed-ended, probing, and reflective questions, leaders can enhance participation, uncover valuable insights, and foster a culture of curiosity and collaboration.

Putting it into Practice

- **Preparation:** Craft questions in advance based on the meeting agenda and objectives to ensure they are relevant and thought-provoking.
- **Active listening:** Show genuine interest in the responses by maintaining eye contact, nodding, and providing verbal acknowledgments. Follow up with additional questions to dig deeper.
- **Body language:** Use non-verbal cues such as leaning forward, maintaining eye contact, and nodding to show engagement and interest. These cues help create a supportive environment that encourages open dialogue and honest responses.

Practice Active Listening

Listening plays a pivotal role in charismatic leadership within the boardroom, shaping how leaders engage with their teams and stakeholders.

Effective listening goes beyond merely hearing words; it involves understanding, empathizing, and responding thoughtfully to others' perspectives and concerns. Here's why being a good listener is crucial for charismatic leadership in the boardroom:

1. **Building Trust and Respect**: Active listening demonstrates genuine interest in others' ideas and opinions. When you actively listen to your team members and stakeholders, you validate their contributions and build trust. This fosters a positive relationship where individuals feel valued and respected, enhancing overall team morale and cohesion.

2. **Fostering Collaboration**: Listening attentively encourages open communication and collaboration. By understanding different viewpoints and considering diverse inputs, teachers can make more informed decisions that reflect the collective wisdom of the team. This collaborative approach not only improves decision-making but also promotes a culture of inclusivity and teamwork within the organization.

3. **Enhancing Problem-Solving**: Effective listening enables teachers to grasp the nuances of complex issues and identify underlying concerns. By actively listening to stakeholders' feedback and concerns, teachers can address challenges more effectively and implement solutions that resonate with the needs of all involved parties.

4. **Empowering Others**: Charismatic teachers empower their teams by listening actively and allowing space for diverse voices to be heard. This inclusive approach motivates team members to contribute their best ideas and innovations, fostering a sense of ownership and commitment to shared goals.

5. **Improving Communication Skills**: Listening is a cornerstone of effective communication. Leaders who prioritize listening skills demonstrate empathy and emotional intelligence, which are essential for building rapport and inspiring others. Clear and empathetic communication contributes to a positive organizational culture and strengthens relationships at all levels.

Studies have shown that leaders who listen actively are perceived as more trustworthy, approachable, and capable of fostering collaborative environments.

(Source: Brownell, 2011; Kouzes & Posner, 2008).

Barriers To Effective Listening

1. **Distractions**: External distractions like noise, interruptions, or multitasking can divert attention from the speaker. To overcome distractions, create a conducive environment by minimizing noise, turning off notifications, and dedicating focused time to listening.
2. **Prejudgments and Assumptions**: Preconceived notions or biases about the speaker or topic can cloud interpretation and hinder active listening. Practice suspending judgment and approaching conversations with an open mind. Focus on understanding the speaker's perspective before forming opinions.
3. **Personal Biases**: Personal biases based on cultural background, experiences, or beliefs may influence how we perceive and interpret information. Awareness of biases is crucial. Actively seek diverse viewpoints and challenge assumptions to foster inclusive listening.

4. **Lack of Empathy**: Empathy involves understanding and sharing the feelings of others. Without empathy, it's challenging to connect deeply with the speaker's emotions and motivations. Practice empathy by actively listening to emotions, acknowledging feelings, and responding with compassion.

5. **Information Overload**: Processing excessive information can overwhelm the listener, leading to selective attention or misunderstanding. Focus on key points, ask for clarification when necessary, and summarize information to ensure comprehension.

Putting it into Practice

- **Eye contact:** Maintain appropriate eye contact to show attentiveness and respect.
- **Nodding:** Use nodding to encourage the speaker and indicate understanding.
- **Reflective listening:** Paraphrase or summarize what the speaker has said to confirm understanding and demonstrate empathy.
- **Avoid interruptions:** Allow the speaker to finish their thoughts without interruptions to ensure they feel heard and respected.

Speak With Structure

Imagine a teacher, Mr. Smith, during a **Parent-Teacher Meeting (PTM).** Mr. Smith stands in front of a group of parents, ready to discuss the academic and behavioral progress of their children.

He starts off by talking about the overall performance of the class: "The students have been doing well overall, but we have some challenges.

Uh, let's see... for instance, we need to improve attendance. Oh, and by the way, we have a field trip next month. Now, regarding your child, Sarah... and yes, sports day is coming up too."

His speech is disorganized, and he constantly switches topics. Parents look puzzled, some whispering among themselves. They are unsure when to ask questions or how to follow the conversation. Mr. Smith notices their confusion but continues in the same erratic manner, leading to a lack of engagement and diminishing the effectiveness of the meeting.

Speaking with structure is crucial for delivering effective boardroom presentations that enhance clarity, persuasiveness, and professionalism. Here's an in-depth explanation of each component:

Importance of Structured Speaking

Structured speaking in boardroom presentations serves several key purposes:

1. **Clarity:** A well-structured presentation ensures that ideas are conveyed in a clear and organized manner, reducing ambiguity and confusion among the audience.
2. **Persuasiveness:** Structured presentations are more persuasive because they guide the audience through a logical flow of information, making it easier for them to follow and accept the speaker's arguments.
3. **Professionalism:** A structured approach reflects professionalism and preparedness, showcasing the speaker's competence and attention to detail.

Components of Structured Speaking

a. Introduction

The introduction sets the stage for the presentation by capturing the audience's attention and providing an overview of what will be covered. Key elements include:

- <u>Attention Grabber:</u> Start with a compelling anecdote, statistic, or thought-provoking question to engage the audience from the outset.
- <u>Thesis Statement:</u> Clearly state the main purpose or objective of the presentation to establish relevance and focus.
- <u>Outline:</u> Provide a brief overview of the main points or topics that will be discussed, giving the audience a roadmap of what to expect.

b. Body

The body of the presentation is where the main content is delivered, organized logically with supporting evidence and examples. Here's how to structure it effectively:

- <u>Logical Flow:</u> Arrange ideas in a logical sequence that builds upon each other, ensuring a smooth transition between points.
- <u>Supporting Evidence:</u> Back up key points with relevant data, examples, case studies, or expert opinions to substantiate arguments and increase credibility.
- <u>Visual Aids:</u> Use charts, graphs, images, or multimedia presentations to enhance understanding and reinforce key points.

c. **Conclusion**

The conclusion serves to reinforce the main message and leave a lasting impression on the audience. Components include:

- <u>Summary</u>: Recap the main points discussed throughout the presentation to reinforce key takeaways.
- <u>Closing Statement</u>: End with a strong and memorable closing statement that reinforces the thesis and leaves the audience with a clear call to action or thought-provoking idea.
- <u>Q&A Preparation:</u> Anticipate potential questions and prepare concise responses to demonstrate thorough knowledge and preparedness.

Techniques to Practice Structure Speaking

Effective techniques such as mind mapping, signposting, and rehearsal play crucial roles in enhancing structured speaking and presentation delivery:

a. **Mind Mapping:** Mind maps visually organize information, helping speakers to structure their thoughts and create a logical flow of ideas. By mapping out key points, connections, and supporting details, speakers can ensure coherence and clarity in their presentation.

This technique not only aids in organizing complex information but also facilitates brainstorming and generating new insights that contribute to a well-rounded presentation structure.

b. **Signposting:** Signposting involves using verbal cues or transitions to guide the audience through different sections of the presentation.

Phrases like "Firstly, secondly, finally," or "Next, let's explore," help listeners anticipate the flow of information and stay engaged. Clear signposting enhances comprehension and retention of key points, ensuring that the audience follows the speaker's train of thought without confusion.

c. **Rehearsal:** Practicing speeches is essential for refining delivery and building confidence. Through rehearsal, speakers familiarize themselves with the content, timing, and transitions of their presentation. This process allows them to adjust pacing, emphasize key messages, and gauge audience reactions. Rehearsal also helps speakers to internalize their material, reducing reliance on notes and enhancing natural delivery, which contributes to a more polished and impactful presentation.

Putting it into Practice

- **Outline and rehearse:** Create a detailed outline of your presentation and rehearse it multiple times to ensure a smooth delivery.
- **Use signposting:** Use clear signposting language (e.g., "Firstly, secondly, finally") to guide the audience through the presentation.
- **Time management:** Allocate appropriate time to each section of your presentation to maintain pace and avoid rushing or running over.

Another place where teachers often spend much of their time—often some of their happiest moments—is the **staffroom**. It's a space where they can express themselves authentically. Let's explore how you can radiate both competence and warmth in the staffroom.

Key Takeaways

- **Engage with anecdotes**: Using relevant and emotionally appealing anecdotes can captivate and persuade your audience.
- **Ask the right questions**: Demonstrating leadership through thoughtful questioning encourages participation and deepens discussions.
- **Practice active listening**: Building trust and respect through active listening fosters a collaborative environment.
- **Speak with structure**: Enhancing clarity and persuasiveness through structured speaking ensures effective communication.
- **Integrate techniques for charisma**: Combining anecdotes, questions, listening, and structured speaking maximizes your impact in the boardroom.

Chapter 9

Influencing The Staffroom

The power of charisma is not in attracting others to you, but in empowering them to believe in themselves.

---- Anonymous

It was a typical afternoon in the bustling staffroom of a school known for its rigorous academic standards and vibrant teacher community. As colleagues mingled over coffee and lesson plans, a new teacher, Ms. Nafisa, caught everyone's attention with her infectious energy and positive presence. Known for her ability to uplift spirits and foster camaraderie, Ms. **Nafisa's** charisma was evident in every interaction.

Charisma plays a pivotal role in cultivating a supportive and collaborative work environment among teachers. Beyond teaching prowess and subject expertise, the ability to inspire and connect with colleagues is crucial for fostering a positive atmosphere where ideas flow freely, teamwork thrives, and collective goals are pursued with enthusiasm.

Ms. Nafisa exemplifies how charisma in the staffroom goes beyond mere social skills—it's about creating a space where teachers feel valued, motivated, and supported. Her ability to uplift colleagues through genuine connections and positive interactions underscores the transformative power of charisma in fostering a cohesive and productive work environment among educators.

In this chapter, we are going to delve into the some tips and tricks to make your interactions with fellow teachers in the staffroom more charismatic.

There are **three steps** to make your interactions in the staffroom charismatic, we are going to delve into them into detail in this chapter.

#1 Make the Other Person A Hero

Have you ever wondered what it feels like to be truly valued in the workplace? Imagine a scenario where your contributions are not just acknowledged but celebrated in a way that makes you feel like a hero.

This concept of making the other person a hero involves recognizing and appreciating colleagues' contributions, strengths, and efforts in a manner that genuinely uplifts and empowers them within the professional environment.

This concept goes beyond mere compliments or recognition—it involves fostering a genuine sense of respect, support, and validation for their work and contributions. Here's a detailed exploration of what it means to make the other person a hero in the workplace:

a. Recognition and Empowerment: Making colleagues feel like heroes involves both recognizing their achievements and empowering them to take meaningful actions. At its core, this approach means openly and sincerely acknowledging their successes, efforts, and unique strengths, whether through public praise in staff meetings or private appreciation in one-on-one conversations. This recognition validates their contributions and motivates them to continue excelling.

Beyond just acknowledgment, it's crucial to empower colleagues by trusting their judgment, supporting their decisions, and providing opportunities for growth and development. When colleagues feel genuinely valued and supported, they are more inclined to engage actively, contribute innovative ideas, and take ownership of their responsibilities. This combination of recognition and empowerment fosters a collaborative and dynamic work environment where everyone feels appreciated and motivated to make significant contributions.

b. Listening and Understanding: A study conducted by Rogers and Farson in 1957 highlights that active listening, which involves giving full attention to the speaker, reflecting on their messages, and responding thoughtfully, contributes significantly to the effectiveness of communication. This approach helps individuals feel valued and respected, as their ideas and concerns are acknowledged and considered. In contrast, passive or superficial listening can lead to misunderstandings, decreased morale, and a lack of trust.

Effective communication plays a crucial role in making colleagues feel like heroes. This includes active listening to their ideas, concerns, and feedback without judgment. When colleagues feel heard and understood, they perceive their contributions as valuable to the team's success. This fosters a culture of openness and collaboration where everyone feels comfortable sharing their thoughts and opinions. Effective communication is central to making colleagues feel like heroes.

One of the most impactful ways to achieve this is through active listening—a process that goes beyond merely hearing words and involves genuinely understanding and valuing the speaker's perspective. Research underscores the significance of active listening in enhancing workplace relationships and fostering a positive work environment.

c. Celebrating Diversity and Inclusivity: Consider a multinational company with a diverse team comprising members from various cultural backgrounds. During a team meeting, the manager highlights the different cultural festivals celebrated by team members, encouraging everyone to share their traditions and experiences. This not only shows respect for each individual's background but also fosters a sense of belonging. For instance, when an employee from India shares a presentation on Diwali traditions, it opens up discussions on cultural diversity, leading to a greater understanding and appreciation among team members. This practice not only makes the employee feel valued but also enriches the team's collective knowledge and fosters a more inclusive environment.

d. Personalized Recognition: I recall a particularly memorable moment when my Principal, **Mrs. Fatima Martin,** surprised me in the staffroom with a gesture that truly touched my heart. It was my birthday, and like any other day, I was going about my usual routine.

The staffroom was bustling with the usual chatter and activity, and I wasn't expecting anything out of the ordinary. Then, out of nowhere, Mrs. Martin walked in, holding a small envelope and a tiny gift box. She approached me with a warm smile, and before I could even process what was happening, she handed me the envelope and the box.

Inside the envelope was a **handwritten note,** carefully crafted in Mrs. Martin's elegant handwriting. The note was filled with kind words and heartfelt appreciation for the work I had been doing. She highlighted specific instances where she had noticed my dedication and mentioned how much she valued my contribution to the school. It wasn't just a generic message; it was clear that she had taken the time to reflect on my efforts and put those thoughts into words.

As I read the note, I felt a surge of pride and gratitude. The words were more than just compliments; they were a validation of the hard work and passion I put into my role. It was as if she had taken a moment to shine a spotlight on my efforts, making me feel like I was truly seen and appreciated.

The surprise didn't end there. Mrs. Martin then asked me to open the small gift box. Inside was a delicate finger ring, simple yet beautiful. It was a thoughtful and personal gift, something that felt uniquely mine. The ring wasn't just a token; it was a symbol of the appreciation and recognition she had for me. It was a reminder that my efforts were noticed and valued, not just by my students or my peers, but by the leadership of the school as well.

This small but incredibly meaningful gesture made me feel like a hero in that moment. It wasn't about the note or the ring alone, but the thoughtfulness behind them. Mrs. Martin had taken the time to acknowledge me in a way that was personal and sincere. It created a lasting impact on me, reinforcing the idea that personalized recognition can truly elevate someone's sense of self-worth and motivation.

Making colleagues feel like heroes is about fostering a culture of appreciation, respect, and empowerment in the workplace. It requires genuine effort to recognize and celebrate their contributions, support their professional growth, and create an inclusive environment where everyone feels valued and motivated to excel.

This experience taught me the power of personalized recognition and how such gestures can transform the way someone feels about their work and their place within an organization. It's a reminder that taking the time to acknowledge someone in a meaningful way can have a profound effect on their morale and their commitment to their role.

Putting it into Practice

- **Regular appreciation rituals:** Establish regular team meetings or email shout-outs to publicly acknowledge and celebrate colleagues' achievements and milestones.
- **Personalized recognition:** Tailor your acknowledgments to each colleague's preferences and achievements. A handwritten note or a personalized message shows genuine appreciation.
- **Offer genuine support:** Actively offer help or resources when colleagues face challenges. Demonstrating solidarity fosters a collaborative environment where everyone feels supported.
- **Practice active listening:** Listen attentively without interrupting, and reflect back on what your colleagues share to show understanding and empathy.
- **Encourage peer recognition:** Foster a culture where colleagues recognize each other's efforts and achievements. This promotes camaraderie and reinforces positive behaviors across the team.

#2 Positive Demeanour And Smile

Maintaining a positive demeanor and consistently smiling in the staffroom is not just about personal happiness; it profoundly influences the overall atmosphere, dynamics, and productivity among colleagues.

Remember how Ms. Nafisa's ever-present smile and positive attitude had a remarkable impact on her colleagues, fostering a supportive and collaborative environment that enhanced team morale and productivity. Here's a detailed exploration of why these traits are crucial and how they contribute to a welcoming and supportive staffroom atmosphere:

Significance of Positive Demeanour and Smiling

When you maintain a positive demeanour and consistently smile in the staffroom, it creates a welcoming environment that fosters openness, approachability, and a sense of belonging among colleagues. It significantly boosts team morale by signalling optimism and resilience, especially in the face of daily challenges in an educational setting. This positivity not only enhances collaboration and communication but also builds trust and stronger professional relationships, encouraging colleagues to engage more openly. Moreover, smiling has the added benefit of improving emotional well-being by reducing stress and promoting a supportive atmosphere where educators feel valued and supported.

Practical Implications and Strategies

a. Consistency in Expression: It's essential to maintain consistency in displaying a positive demeanor and smiling, even during challenging times. This consistency reinforces the message of resilience and optimism, serving as a beacon of positivity for colleagues.

b. Active Listening and Empathy: Combine smiling with active listening and empathy to demonstrate genuine interest in colleagues' thoughts and feelings. This holistic approach not only promotes positive interactions but also strengthens bonds by showing respect and understanding.

c. Celebrating Successes: Use moments of shared success or achievement to amplify positivity in the staffroom. Celebrating milestones, no matter how small, reinforces a culture of positivity and appreciation among colleagues.

d. Managing Stress and Challenges: During stressful periods or when facing challenges, maintain a positive outlook and encourage colleagues to approach difficulties with optimism and teamwork. A smile during these times can serve as a reminder of resilience and collective strength.

e. Greeting And Approachabilty: To enhance greeting and approachability in the staffroom, start conversations with warmth and positivity by using personalized greetings and inquiring about colleagues' well-being. A smile and direct eye contact convey sincerity, encouraging comfortable interactions. Initiating small talk on light-hearted topics helps build rapport and create a friendly atmosphere before moving on to more serious discussions.

f. Body Language: To foster effective communication in the staffroom, maintain open and welcoming body language. Keep an open posture, avoiding crossed arms or legs, to appear approachable. Use facial expressions like smiling and nodding to convey interest and empathy. Lean slightly forward during conversations to show attentiveness, demonstrating respect and encouraging open dialogue.

g Handling Stress And Challenges: Maintain composure in stressful situations. Practice mindfulness techniques like deep breathing to stay calm. Focus on finding solutions collaboratively with colleagues rather than dwelling on problems, maintaining a proactive and positive mindset. Don't hesitate to seek support from colleagues or mentors when needed, building a network for guidance and resilience.

Maintaining a positive demeanour and smiling in the staffroom is not merely a superficial gesture; it's a powerful tool for creating a welcoming, supportive, and productive environment among colleagues.

By integrating these practices into daily interactions, educators not only enhance their own professional relationships but also contribute to a collaborative culture where everyone feels supported and motivated to achieve common goals.

Putting it into Practice

- **Start with a genuine smile:** Begin each day with a smile that reflects warmth and positivity. Greet colleagues with sincerity, using their names to personalize interactions.
- **Practice active listening:** Engage in conversations attentively by maintaining eye contact and nodding to show understanding. Reflect on what others say to demonstrate empathy and foster deeper connections.
- **Maintain open body language:** Keep your posture relaxed and open, avoiding crossed arms or closed gestures. This non-verbal cue invites others to approach you and facilitates more relaxed and open communication.
- **Initiate positive conversations:** Lead discussions with topics that inspire optimism and camaraderie. Share uplifting stories or achievements to create a supportive atmosphere.

- **Handle stress positively:** During challenging moments, maintain composure by taking deep breaths and focusing on solutions. Seek support from colleagues when needed, promoting a culture of mutual assistance and resilience.

#3 Avoiding Small Talk

In the bustling staffroom of a high school, where conversations often drifted into trivialities about weekend plans or the latest office gossip, I noticed a significant shift when we decided to focus on more substantive discussions.

One day, rather than engaging in the usual small talk about the weather or upcoming events, a colleague brought up a new teaching strategy she had been experimenting with. This shift sparked an engaging discussion about innovative approaches to teaching, leading to a fruitful exchange of ideas and strategies that benefited everyone involved.

Reducing meaningless small talk in the staffroom can significantly enhance the quality of communication and foster respect among colleagues. Small talk often fills the silence but rarely contributes to meaningful relationships or professional growth. By shifting focus to more substantive discussions, you can build stronger connections, share valuable insights, and support each other's development. Meaningful conversations encourage mutual respect and understanding, which are crucial for a cohesive and supportive work environment. They also stimulate intellectual engagement, leading to more productive and satisfying interactions.

By avoiding small talk and encouraging meaningful conversations, you can create a staffroom culture that is more respectful, intellectually stimulating, and supportive.

Let's see how we can encourage meaningful conversations with our colleagues in the staffroom:

Initiating Relevant Discussions

Starting conversations on topics that matter can be a powerful way to move beyond small talk. Here are some strategies to spark meaningful discussions:

a. Identify Common Interests: Find topics that resonate with your colleagues, such as recent educational trends, classroom management strategies, or innovative teaching methods. This can be done by paying attention to what colleagues often talk about or express interest in during meetings or informal chats.

b. Ask Thought-Provoking Questions: Instead of generic questions, ask open-ended ones that require deeper thinking. For example, "What's a teaching strategy that has significantly improved your classroom dynamics?" or "How do you handle student motivation in your classes?"

c. Share Experiences: Lead by example and share your own experiences, challenges, and successes. This openness can encourage others to share their stories and create a more engaged and collaborative atmosphere.

d. Bring Up Current Events: Discussing recent developments in education, such as policy changes or technological advancements, can provide a rich source of conversation that is both relevant and intellectually stimulating.

e. Create Opportunities for Dialogue: Propose regular discussion groups or informal meet-ups focused on professional topics. This can give everyone a chance to engage in deeper conversations in a structured yet relaxed setting.

Sharing Insights

Once a meaningful conversation is initiated, contributing valuable insights can further enrich the dialogue. Here's how you can do that effectively:

a. **Prepare in Advance:** Stay informed about the latest trends and research in education. This preparation will enable you to share relevant information and insights during discussions.

b. **Be Authentic:** Share your genuine thoughts and experiences. Authenticity builds trust and encourages others to open up as well.

c. **Ask for Opinions:** After sharing your insight, invite others to share their perspectives. Questions like "What do you think about this approach?" or "Have you tried something similar?" can foster a more inclusive conversation.

d. **Build on Ideas:** Instead of just waiting for your turn to speak, actively listen and build on what others say. This collaborative approach can lead to more comprehensive and innovative ideas.

e. **Use Examples:** When presenting an idea or insight, back it up with examples from your own experience or relevant case studies. This makes your contributions more concrete and relatable.

Putting it into Practice

- **Set intentions:** Before entering the staffroom, set a personal intention to engage in meaningful conversation rather than small talk.

- **Focus on quality:** Aim for quality over quantity in your interactions. Even short, meaningful exchanges can be more impactful than prolonged small talk.

- **Listen actively:** Show genuine interest in what your colleagues are saying. Active listening encourages others to share more deeply and fosters mutual respect.

- **Use transitional phrases:** If a conversation veers into small talk, use transitional phrases to steer it back to more substantive topics. For example, "That's interesting! It reminds me of a challenge I faced in my class recently. How do you handle…?"

- **Follow-Up:** After an initial meaningful conversation, follow up in future interactions. This continuity demonstrates that you value the exchange and are invested in ongoing professional dialogue.

#4 Additional Strategies for Charisma in Staffroom

Charisma is a vital attribute for teachers, not only in the classroom but also in staffroom interactions. To create a positive, collaborative, and productive environment, teachers can employ several strategies to enhance their charisma. Here are some key approaches:

a. Conflict Resolution

Effectively resolving conflicts in the staffroom enhances a harmonious atmosphere and boosts your charisma. Start by actively listening to all parties without interruption, showing empathy to de-escalate tensions. Maintain neutrality to foster trust and encourage open dialogue. Focus on finding solutions rather than assigning blame, and follow up with involved parties to ensure the resolution is effective. Demonstrating leadership in conflict resolution contributes to a positive workplace environment.

b. Building Trust

Building trust in the staffroom is essential for fostering a supportive and collaborative environment. Be transparent in your communications, share relevant information, and be honest about your intentions. Consistently follow through on commitments to demonstrate reliability.

Show respect for colleagues' ideas, opinions, and time, and maintain confidentiality with sensitive information. These actions enhance your credibility, strengthen professional relationships, and contribute to your overall charisma.

c. Celebrating Successes

Celebrating successes, both individual and collective, significantly boosts morale and motivation. Publicly recognizing achievements during meetings or newsletters highlights the value of colleagues' efforts. Personal appreciation through thank-you notes or direct congratulations shows genuine care. Organizing team-building activities and encouraging peer recognition fosters a sense of community and mutual support. These practices contribute to a positive work environment and enhance your charisma.

d. Continuous Improvement

Charisma can be developed and enhanced through continuous improvement. Engage in professional development by attending workshops and seminars on interpersonal skills and leadership. Regularly seek feedback from colleagues and supervisors to identify areas for growth.

Practice self-reflection to understand your strengths and areas needing improvement. Finding a mentor for guidance and applying learned skills in daily interactions also helps refine your charisma.

e. Conscious Mirroring

Conscious mirroring involves subtly reflecting a colleague's body language, tone, and communication style to foster empathy and rapport. To implement this, mirror their posture and gestures naturally, align with their tone and pace of speech, and actively listen by paraphrasing their points. This technique enhances interpersonal connections, reduces social barriers, and improves communication effectiveness, creating a more collaborative and comfortable environment.

f. Personal Space

Respecting personal space is crucial for maintaining a positive work environment. To do this, observe non-verbal cues to gauge comfort levels and adjust your proximity accordingly, typically maintaining an arm's length distance. Avoid unnecessary physical contact and be mindful of boundaries. Respecting personal space promotes comfort, reduces anxiety, and fosters a professional atmosphere, ensuring that all colleagues feel secure and valued.

By committing to continuous improvement, you can enhance your interpersonal skills and maintain a high level of charisma, contributing to a positive and dynamic staffroom environment.

I encourage every teacher to embrace these strategies and actively integrate them into their daily interactions with colleagues. Start by practicing active listening and showing empathy, much like Ms. Nafisa's ability to connect with each student uniquely. Recognize and celebrate your peers' achievements, creating a culture where successes are highlighted and motivation flourishes. Build trust through transparency, reliability, and respect, while maintaining a positive demeanour and approachability, akin to Ms. Nafisa's uplifting presence in the staffroom.

Let's work together to create a staffroom where every teacher feels valued, supported, and inspired, just as Ms. Nafisa's approach made each parent and student feel special.

Key Takeaways

- **Value and recognition**: Acknowledge and praise your colleagues' contributions to foster a supportive and collaborative staffroom atmosphere.
- **Positive demeanour**: Maintaining a positive attitude and smiling can significantly enhance communication and create a welcoming environment for all staff members.
- **Meaningful conversations**: Avoiding small talk and encouraging discussions on relevant topics can lead to more productive and respectful interactions among colleagues.
- **Active listening and trust**: Building trust through active listening, transparency, and honesty is crucial for creating a harmonious and effective staffroom dynamic.

Chapter 10

Mastering In Parent-Teacher Meetings

I am real tall when I stand on my charisma.

Harlan Ellison

Parent-teacher meetings used to be a daunting experience for me, akin to the dreaded Monday morning huddle described in Chapter 8. In Dubai, where parents are seen as the ultimate clients, teachers often find themselves in a tough spot. Despite being the professional in the room, you sometimes feel powerless when parents come in with their complaints and concerns. It was a regular occurrence for me to face a barrage of grievances with little to no appreciation, and the meetings often left me feeling disheartened.

The **turning point** came when I attended my own child's parent-teacher meeting. As a high school teacher, I had always been on the other side of these meetings. However, when I visited my daughter's kindergarten teacher, I was struck by a different experience. The teacher greeted my daughter with a warm high-five, engaged her in a friendly conversation, and made her feel valued. This positive, personal touch made me feel more receptive to the teacher's feedback, even though it included both positives and areas for improvement.

Inspired by this encounter, I decided to apply a similar approach in my own parent-teacher meetings. I began by connecting with the students personally and offering genuine compliments. This simple shift in strategy transformed the atmosphere of the meetings. Parents, who previously might have come in with a list of complaints, were more receptive and appreciative. By focusing on positive interactions and genuine engagement, I found that I could handle complaints more effectively and maintain a constructive dialogue.

This approach not only made the meetings more pleasant but also helped me overcome my previous dread of these interactions. By incorporating a balance of genuine praise and constructive feedback, I was able to foster a more positive environment and strengthen my relationships with both students and their parents.

Parent-teacher meetings serve as a bridge between the home and school environment. These meetings provide a platform for teachers and parents to discuss a child's academic progress, behavioral development, and overall well-being. They are essential not only for addressing concerns and celebrating achievements but also for collaboratively setting goals and strategies to support the student's growth. Effective communication during these meetings ensures that both parents and teachers are aligned in their expectations and efforts, creating a supportive network that significantly benefits the student's learning experience.

As educators, our role extends beyond delivering curriculum content to fostering strong partnerships with parents. To achieve this, adopting effective communication strategies is crucial.

This chapter focuses on three key strategies to enhance charisma and effectiveness during parent-teacher meetings. Let us delve onto it one by one.

1. **Be Assertive**

Assertiveness is the ability to express oneself clearly, confidently, and respectfully, while valuing both your own needs and those of others. In the context of parent-teacher meetings, assertiveness means communicating your observations, concerns, and suggestions about a student's performance in a manner that is direct yet considerate. It involves stating your points clearly without ambiguity and confidently addressing any issues that arise while also being open to parents' perspectives.

By balancing confidence with respect, assertive communication helps in navigating potentially challenging conversations with parents, ultimately contributing to more productive and supportive discussions regarding a student's development.

Techniques for Assertive Communication

a. Clear Language

Using clear and specific language is fundamental to assertive communication. When discussing a student's performance, avoid vague terms and generalizations. Instead, use precise and unambiguous words to convey your observations and concerns. For instance, rather than saying, *"Your child needs to improve in math,"* specify the areas that need attention: *"Your child has difficulty with multiplication and division."* This clarity helps parents understand the exact issues and what steps need to be taken to address them. Additionally, clear language reduces the risk of misunderstandings and ensures that your message is received as intended.

b. Positive Body Language

Positive body language is essential in reinforcing your verbal communication and conveying confidence. An open posture, such as standing or sitting with your shoulders back and arms relaxed, indicates that you are approachable and ready to engage in a constructive conversation. Steady eye contact shows that you are attentive and sincere in your communication, which helps in building trust with parents. Controlled gestures, such as using your hands to emphasize points without being overly animated, can also aid in illustrating your points effectively. By aligning your body language with your verbal messages, you can create a cohesive and powerful communication style that enhances your assertiveness.

c. Calm Tone

Maintaining a steady and calm tone of voice is crucial in assertive communication. A calm tone helps to convey confidence and control, which reassures parents that you are knowledgeable and capable of handling the situation. It is important to avoid raising your voice or allowing your tone to become harsh, as this can create tension and defensiveness. Instead, aim for a balanced tone that is firm yet friendly, showing that you are serious about the topic but also open to dialogue. Practicing deep breathing and staying mindful of your emotions can help you maintain this calm demeanor, even in potentially stressful discussions.

Scenarios and Examples of Assertive Communication

Example 1: Addressing Concerns About a Student's Behavior Assertively

Imagine you need to discuss a student's disruptive behavior in class with their parents. Start by clearly stating the specific behavior you have observed. For instance:

"Mr. and Mrs. Smith, I've noticed that John often talks during lessons and distracts his classmates. This behavior has been recurring over the past month and is impacting his and others' learning experience."

Use positive body language by maintaining steady eye contact and keeping an open posture. Continue with a calm and steady tone:

"I understand that children sometimes act out for various reasons, and I believe we can work together to find a solution. I'd like to explore some strategies that could help John focus better in class, such as a behavior chart or regular check-ins with me. What are your thoughts on this?"

By clearly describing the behavior, demonstrating openness to collaboration, and proposing specific solutions, you assertively address the issue without being confrontational or accusatory.

Example 2: Discussing Academic Performance Without Sounding Defensive or Accusatory

Suppose you need to discuss a student's declining grades in Math. Begin by using clear language to explain the situation:

"Mrs. Johnson, I want to talk about Emma's recent math tests. Over the past two months, her scores have dropped from Bs to Cs, particularly in algebra and geometry."

Maintain positive body language, such as an open posture and controlled gestures, to show you are approachable and focused. Use a calm tone to convey your points:

"I know Emma is capable, and I want to help her get back on track. I've noticed she struggles with problem-solving steps. Could we discuss some

strategies, such as additional practice at home or after-school tutoring, to support her improvement?"

By focusing on specific areas of concern and suggesting practical solutions, you assertively communicate the issue while respecting the parent's perspective and avoiding any defensiveness or accusations.

Putting it into Practice

- **Preparation:** Preparing notes and key points beforehand ensures you cover all important topics and maintain focus. This helps in delivering a structured and confident discussion.
- **Active listening:** Acknowledge parents' concerns by nodding and summarizing their points. This shows respect and understanding, fostering a collaborative atmosphere.
- **Staying on track:** Keep the conversation focused on the student's progress and potential solutions. This helps avoid distractions and ensures a productive meeting.
- **Empathy:** Show empathy by expressing understanding of the parents' feelings and perspectives. Statements like "I can see why this is concerning for you" can build trust and rapport.
- **Follow-up plan:** End the meeting with a clear follow-up plan, outlining the next steps and setting a date for the next check-in. This demonstrates your commitment to the student's development and reassures parents of ongoing support.

Common Pitfalls and How to Avoid Them

- Over-Aggressiveness: To stay assertive without being confrontational, maintain a calm tone and open body language.

Avoid raising your voice or using harsh language. Instead, focus on expressing your points clearly and respectfully.

- Passivity: Avoid meek responses that can undermine your authority by using firm and specific language. Practice saying "I" statements to assert your position without sounding apologetic, and ensure your body language supports your verbal message with steady eye contact and an upright posture

The 'But' Syndrome

The word **"but"** often negates everything said before it, creating a psychological barrier in communication. When we use "but," it can unintentionally dismiss or undermine the positive or conciliatory statements that precede it. **For example**, saying *"You did well on your test, but you need to improve your homework"* can make the listener focus only on the negative aspect, overshadowing the initial praise.

This can be particularly problematic in parent-teacher meetings, where building a collaborative and positive relationship is crucial. Instead of feeling encouraged by the feedback, parents may perceive the teacher as critical or unsupportive.

Psychologically, "but" signals a contrast or opposition, which can create defensiveness or disappointment in the listener.

By avoiding **'but,'** and using alternative structures like **'and'** or rephrasing sentences to maintain positivity, we can foster a more constructive and engaging dialogue. This approach helps to ensure that feedback is received as intended, promoting improvement while maintaining a supportive atmosphere.

Techniques to Avoid 'But'

Let me help you with some techniques I use to avoid the 'but' in my interactions during parent-teacher meetings:

a. **Using 'And':** One effective substitute for "but" is "and." This simple change can transform a potentially negative statement into a constructive one.

   For example, instead of saying, *"You did well on your test, but you need to improve your homework,"* you can say, *"You did well on your test, **and** I believe you can also improve your homework with some additional effort."*

   This way, you acknowledge the achievement and suggest an area for improvement without negating the initial praise.

b. **Using 'However':** Another alternative is "however." While it still indicates a contrast, it is softer and less likely to negate the previous statement.

   For instance, *"You did well on your test; **however**, there's room for improvement in your homework."*

   The pause before 'however' helps to separate the two thoughts, making the feedback feel more balanced.

c. **Pausing:** Sometimes, a strategic pause can replace 'but' effectively. Instead of connecting two contrasting statements with "but," try stating the positive point, pausing for a moment, and then continuing with the constructive feedback.

For example, *"You did well on your test. (**Pause**) I also noticed that there's room for improvement in your homework."*

d. **Positive Framing**: Craft sentences that maintain a positive tone and coherence without contradiction.

For instance, instead of *"You did well on your test, but your homework is lacking," rephrase it to, "Your test results were impressive, and with a bit more focus on your homework, you can excel even further."*

This approach frames the feedback as a continuation of the positive statement, encouraging improvement without diminishing the achievement.

e. **Balancing Feedback**: Ensure that feedback is balanced by providing specific praise followed by constructive suggestions.

For example, *"I was really impressed with your test performance. To reach the same level in your homework, let's work on developing a consistent study routine."*

This method emphasizes growth and progress rather than pointing out shortcomings.

f. **Encouraging Language**: Use encouraging language that promotes a growth mindset. Replace "but" with phrases that emphasize potential and improvement.

For instance, *"You've shown great progress in your tests, and I know that with a bit more effort, your homework will reflect the same improvement."*

g. **Clarifying Expectations**: Clearly outline expectations and provide actionable steps for improvement. Instead of saying, *"You did well on your test, but your homework needs work,"* **you can say,** *"Your test scores are a testament to your abilities. Let's apply the same strategies to your homework by setting aside dedicated time each day for practice."*

h. **Expressing Confidence**: Show confidence in the student's ability to improve.

For example, *"You've done a fantastic job on your test. I'm confident that with the same dedication, you'll see great results in your homework as well."* This reinforces belief in the student's capabilities and encourages a positive attitude towards improvement.

Rephrased Feedback Versions

Consider a scenario where a student's academic performance is generally good, but they are struggling with math. A traditional approach might be,

"Your grades in English and Science are excellent, but you need to improve in Math." This statement, although truthful, can diminish the praise and focus on the negative.

Rephrased: *"Your grades in English and science are excellent, and I can see that you're putting in a lot of effort. To help you achieve the same success in math, let's explore some additional resources and study techniques that might work for you."*

This rephrasing acknowledges the student's strengths and presents the area of improvement as a manageable challenge, fostering a growth mindset.

In a situation where a student exhibits good participation in class but sometimes disrupts others, a typical statement might be,

"You participate well in class, but you need to stop disrupting your classmates." This approach may make the student feel their positive contributions are overshadowed by their negative behavior.

Rephrased: *"I really appreciate how actively you participate in class discussions. Your insights add a lot of value. To make sure everyone benefits from a focused learning environment, let's work on finding ways to express your enthusiasm without disrupting others. How about we discuss some strategies together?"*

Putting it into Practice

- **Mindful speaking**: Be conscious of your language choices during meetings. Instead of automatically using "but," pause and think about how to convey your message positively and constructively.
- **Positive framing**: Always highlight strengths before discussing areas of improvement. This approach ensures that parents and students feel recognized for their achievements while also understanding where they can grow.
- **Practice**: Regularly practice rephrasing statements to avoid using "but." This will help make positive communication a natural habit.
- **Active listening**: Pay close attention to parents' concerns and feedback. This helps in crafting responses that are empathetic and avoid negating their feelings or observations.

- **Consistent feedback**: Provide regular, balanced feedback that incorporates positive reinforcement alongside constructive criticism. This builds a habit of positive communication and minimizes the reliance on negating conjunctions like "but."

3. The Feedback Sandwich

The feedback sandwich is a communication technique used to deliver constructive feedback in a balanced and encouraging manner. It involves "**sandwiching**" the constructive criticism between two positive comments. This method helps to soften the impact of the critique, making it more palatable and motivating for the recipient.

The feedback sandwich consists of three layers and let us delve into each of them.

Components of a Feedback Sandwich

This method is structured around three key components: a positive start, constructive feedback, and a positive end. Each component plays a crucial role in ensuring that the feedback is received well and prompts meaningful improvement.

a. Positive Start

The feedback sandwich begins with a genuine positive comment. This initial praise serves several purposes: it sets a constructive tone for the conversation, acknowledges the recipient's strengths, and builds rapport. For instance, in a parent-teacher meeting, a teacher might start by praising a student's enthusiasm for learning or their recent improvement in a specific area. This approach helps to create a supportive atmosphere and makes the recipient more receptive to the subsequent feedback. The key is to ensure that the praise is sincere and specific, rather than generic or exaggerated. Genuine acknowledgment of achievements fosters a sense of validation and encourages the recipient to be open to further discussion.

b. Constructive Feedback

Following the positive start, the next step is to provide constructive feedback. This component involves addressing areas that need improvement in a clear, respectful, and actionable manner. It's important to be specific and focus on behaviors or actions rather than personal attributes. For example, instead of saying, *"You need to improve,"* a teacher might say, *"I've noticed that completing assignments on time has been a challenge. Developing a schedule might help manage time better."* This clarity helps the recipient understand what changes are needed and why they are important. Constructive feedback should be delivered in a way that maintains the recipient's dignity and encourages their development, avoiding blame or negativity.

c. Positive End

The feedback sandwich concludes with another positive note to reinforce encouragement and support. This final component is designed to uplift the recipient and reaffirm their potential for growth. For instance, the teacher might end by expressing confidence in the student's ability to improve and highlighting another area where they are excelling. This positive reinforcement helps to balance the conversation, ensuring that the recipient feels valued and motivated rather than discouraged. Ending on an encouraging note helps to maintain a positive relationship and reinforces the overall supportive nature of the feedback.

By starting and ending on a positive note while clearly addressing areas for improvement, the feedback sandwich fosters a constructive and supportive dialogue that promotes growth and development.

#Scenario 1: Academic Feedback

Imagine a parent-teacher meeting where a teacher needs to address a student's inconsistent performance in mathematics. The feedback sandwich could be applied as follows:

- <u>Positive Start:</u> *"I want to start by acknowledging the tremendous effort Sarah has put into her math assignments this semester. Her enthusiasm for the subject and willingness to participate in class discussions have been impressive."*
- <u>Constructive Feedback:</u> *"However, I've noticed that Sarah struggles with applying the concepts during tests, which affects her overall grades. It might be helpful for her to work on some additional practice problems at home or attend a few extra help sessions. This extra support could reinforce her understanding and boost her confidence."*
- <u>Positive End:</u> *"Despite these challenges, Sarah's curiosity and dedication are her greatest assets. With some additional practice, I'm confident she will see significant improvements. Her positive attitude toward learning is a strong foundation for overcoming these obstacles."*

This approach balances praise with practical suggestions, helping to motivate the student while clearly outlining areas for improvement.

Scenario 2: Behavioral Feedback

Consider a scenario where a teacher needs to address a student's disruptive behavior in class:

- Positive Start: *"I appreciate how James has been contributing actively during group activities and showing enthusiasm in his work. His creativity and participation are valued in our classroom."*
- Constructive Feedback: *"However, there have been a few instances where his outbursts have disrupted the flow of the lesson. It's important for James to practice waiting his turn and raising his hand before speaking. This will help maintain a positive and focused learning environment for everyone."*
- Positive End: *"I believe that with some guidance on managing his behavior, James can continue to be a positive and influential presence in the class. His ability to engage with the material is a strong point, and I look forward to seeing his continued progress."*

Putting it into Practice

- **Authenticity:** Ensure that positive comments are genuine and specific. Avoid generic praise; instead, highlight specific achievements or improvements to reinforce sincerity and impact.
- **Clarity:** Make sure constructive feedback is clear and actionable. Provide concrete examples of what needs to be improved and suggest practical steps for achieving those improvements.
- **Balance:** Maintain a balance between positive and constructive comments. Avoid overloading the feedback with criticism; instead, ensure that each piece of constructive feedback is framed within a context of overall positive reinforcement.

- **Timing:** Deliver feedback in a timely manner. Provide feedback as soon as possible after the observed behavior or performance to ensure it is relevant and actionable.
- **Follow-up:** Plan a follow-up discussion to review progress. After delivering the feedback sandwich, schedule a future meeting or check-in to assess improvements and offer additional support if needed.

Common Pitfalls and How to Avoid Them

Avoid insincerity by ensuring that positive comments are specific and genuinely reflect the student's achievements, rather than being vague or generic. At the same time, be mindful not to overemphasize praise to the point where it overshadows the constructive feedback. Striking a balance ensures that the student feels supported while also understanding the areas that need improvement for their overall development.

In summary, mastering the art of effective communication during parent-teacher meetings is crucial for fostering strong relationships with parents and supporting student growth. Being assertive allows teachers to express their views confidently while maintaining respect for parents' perspectives. Avoiding the word **'but'** helps keep conversations constructive and positive, ensuring that feedback is received in the best possible light. Utilizing the feedback sandwich technique ensures that constructive criticism is delivered in a balanced manner, reinforcing positive behaviors and encouraging improvement.

I encourage you to apply these strategies in your next parent-teacher meeting to enhance your communication effectiveness. By being clear and respectful, avoiding negative language, and providing balanced feedback, you can build stronger partnerships with parents and contribute to better student outcomes. As we approach the end of this book, get ready to understand the true essence of charisma in teaching in the upcoming chapter. It emphasizes the development of charisma for the betterment of teaching and creating a positive impact.

Key Takeaways

- **Assertive communication:** Maintain clear, confident, and respectful dialogue to establish authority and professionalism.
- **Positive language:** Avoid using "but" to ensure that feedback is received positively and constructively.
- **Feedback Sandwich:** Use the feedback sandwich method to balance praise and constructive criticism, fostering motivation and improvement.
- **Preparation and practice:** Prepare thoroughly for meetings and practice communication techniques to enhance effectiveness.
- **Active listening and adaptability:** Listen actively to parents' concerns and be flexible in your approach to cater to individual preferences and needs.

Chapter 11

Charisma With Integrity

Charisma without character is postponed calamity.
---- **Peter Ajisafe**

As I sit here reflecting on everything we've explored in this book, I find myself coming back to one simple truth: charisma, at its core, isn't just about dazzling people or making a memorable impression. It's about connection, impact, and purpose. It

Charisma, in its truest form, is inseparable from character. I've seen it firsthand—teachers who are naturally charismatic aren't simply the ones who speak the loudest or stand out the most. They're the ones who remain grounded in their values, and whose words and actions consistently reflect integrity. Their charisma isn't a tool to draw attention to themselves, but a way to better connect with their students and colleagues. It's authentic because it stems from who they truly are.

I've encountered individuals who radiate charisma yet remain humble, kind, and true to their core beliefs. They don't seek admiration for the sake of it—they aim to inspire, to lift others up. These teachers make a lasting impression, not because they demand it, but because their integrity shines through in every interaction. This kind of charisma, built on a solid ethical foundation, is what I've always aspired to cultivate in myself and encourage in others.

Charisma without character, on the other hand, is hollow. It can easily become manipulative, superficial, and disingenuous. I've seen it happen—

where someone might try to project confidence or charm but lacks the values to back it up. It quickly falls apart because students and colleagues can sense when something isn't genuine. In teaching, this disconnect can erode trust and create an atmosphere of uncertainty.

As we reach the conclusion of this practical guide on charisma, let's explore the various types of charisma and how we can embody different forms of it in various situations.

1. Focus Charisma—The Power of Undivided Attention

Focus charisma is one of the most powerful forms of charisma, and its essence lies in the ability to be fully present with the people around you. It's about making someone feel like they are the most important person in the room, even if only for a few moments. In the context of teaching, focus charisma means offering students your undivided attention, making them feel heard and valued. When you give students your complete focus, you convey respect and care, which in turn fosters deeper connections and trust. This can be transformative, as students who feel valued are more likely to engage in learning, take risks, and push themselves to grow.

In the staffroom, focus charisma is equally powerful. Giving a colleague your full attention, whether during a casual conversation or a more formal discussion, signals that you respect their perspective. It strengthens relationships and can even influence how you are perceived as a leader. Colleagues and administrators will be drawn to you because your focus and attentiveness make them feel valued, and people are naturally attracted to those who make them feel significant. In meetings or staff discussions, being the person who listens intently and responds thoughtfully can increase your influence and create a positive ripple effect within the school community.

However, as with all forms of charisma, focus charisma must be aligned with integrity. When rooted in character, focus charisma is about genuinely wanting to understand and support others, rather than using your attention as a tool for manipulation. It is easy to fall into the trap of using this kind of charisma to gain approval or curry favor, but that approach ultimately undermines its power.

The aim of focus charisma is not to be liked or to win people over superficially, but to build authentic connections based on trust and respect.

One powerful example of focus charisma is **Barack Obama**. Known for his calm and composed demeanor, Obama often displayed focus charisma in his interactions with both world leaders and ordinary citizens. When speaking with someone, he had a remarkable ability to make that person feel as though they were the only individual in the room, giving them his undivided attention. This quality made people feel heard and valued, fostering trust and deepening connections.

2. Visionary Charisma—Inspiring with a Greater Purpose

Visionary charisma is the ability to inspire and energize others by sharing a compelling vision or goal. It's about painting a picture of what could be and motivating others to work towards that future.

In the realm of education, visionary charisma can be a powerful tool. For teachers, it means more than just teaching a curriculum; it involves inspiring students with a broader perspective on their learning journey. Imagine a teacher who not only explains the importance of a subject but also connects it to real-world applications, future careers, and personal growth. This approach helps students see the value in what they're learning and motivates them to engage more deeply with the material. Similarly, when working with colleagues, a teacher with visionary charisma can articulate a shared goal for the school or a new teaching initiative, sparking excitement and commitment among the staff.

However, for visionary charisma to be truly impactful, it must be anchored in authenticity and aligned with one's core values. It's not about presenting an idealized dream that sounds impressive but fails to reflect the reality or your true beliefs. An authentic vision is one that genuinely represents your values and aspirations, and is pursued with integrity.

When teachers articulate a vision that is deeply rooted in their own values, it resonates more strongly with students and colleagues. It demonstrates that the vision is not just a transient idea but a genuine aspiration that they are committed to achieving.

A prime example of visionary charisma is **Nelson Mandela.** His vision for a united, democratic South Africa—free from the divisions of apartheid—was not just a political goal but a deeply personal commitment to equality and justice. Mandela's charisma came from his ability to inspire hope, even during the darkest times, and to communicate a clear and inclusive vision for the future. His authenticity and unwavering belief in this vision fostered trust, not only among his supporters but also among those who once opposed him. This made his vision more compelling and achievable, as he led South Africa toward reconciliation and unity.

3. Kindness Charisma—Charisma with Compassion

Kindness charisma is connecting with others through genuine empathy and compassion. It goes beyond superficial gestures of kindness, focusing on creating meaningful connections by truly understanding and addressing the emotional needs of others.

In the classroom, kindness charisma can transform the learning environment. Teachers who exhibit kindness charisma are able to create a space where students feel safe and supported. For instance, a teacher who takes the time to understand each student's unique challenges and strengths, who offers encouragement during difficult times, and who celebrates their successes with genuine enthusiasm fosters an atmosphere of trust and respect.

Beyond the classroom, kindness charisma can significantly impact interactions with colleagues and the broader school community. A teacher who demonstrates kindness charisma by actively listening to colleagues' concerns, offering support during challenging times, and celebrating others' achievements contributes to a positive and collaborative work environment. This approach can help build strong professional relationships and a cohesive team, which is essential for creating a productive and harmonious school culture.

When kindness is rooted in sincerity, it builds deep and lasting connections. People feel valued and respected, knowing that the kindness they receive is genuine and not a calculated gesture.

For instance, a teacher who consistently shows compassion and empathy, even in small, everyday interactions, creates an environment where trust and mutual respect flourish. This authentic approach not only strengthens relationships but also fosters a culture where kindness and support are integral to the community's values.

4. Authority Charisma—Commanding Respect with Integrity

Authority charisma is the ability to project confidence, competence, and control in a way that commands respect. It's not just about holding a position of power but about embodying qualities that inspire trust and admiration from others. This form of charisma is essential for leaders and educators who need to maintain respect and ensure effective management without resorting to fear or intimidation.

For teachers, authority charisma plays a crucial role in creating a well-structured and respectful classroom environment. It involves projecting confidence and competence in your role, which helps establish your position as a knowledgeable and reliable authority figure. For instance, when a teacher confidently delivers lessons, manages classroom behavior effectively, and addresses issues with clarity and fairness, students are more likely to respect and follow their lead.

Balancing authority with approachability is key. A teacher who projects authority while remaining approachable fosters a positive learning environment where students feel respected but also comfortable seeking help and engaging in open dialogue. This balance is achieved by demonstrating fairness, actively listening to students' concerns, and showing empathy, which helps maintain a supportive atmosphere while upholding standards and expectations.

True authority charisma is rooted in integrity. It's essential that authority is not wielded through dominance or intimidation but through competence, fairness, and consistency. When authority is aligned with one's core values, it becomes a natural extension of one's character rather than a façade for control.

For example, a teacher who consistently applies rules with fairness and respects students' individual needs is seen as a just authority figure. Such an approach earns genuine respect and fosters a positive learning environment where students feel valued and motivated.

Charisma with Character: Bringing it altogether

As I am writing this chapter today, I can't help but reflect on whether achieving "Charisma with Character" is an uphill task. The more I think about it, the more I realize that it's not just a significant quality—it's a non-negotiable trait for anyone in a leadership role, especially as a teacher. It's not about charm for the sake of appearances but about a deep alignment of charisma with one's values and integrity.

Looking back on my own journey, I am reminded of someone who embodied this principle effortlessly—Ms. Mukta Bakshi, our Primary School Head. She had an extraordinary ability to switch between different types of charisma depending on the situation. When faced with a challenge or the need to demonstrate a new concept to the teaching staff, she would tap into her focus charisma, honing in on the issue with laser-like clarity. Her presence in those moments was magnetic, drawing everyone's attention and inspiring confidence in her leadership.

Yet, Ms. Bakshi was equally adept at showing kindness charisma. I vividly remember how she would instinctively offer solace and support to any teacher going through a stressful time. Her empathy wasn't performative or superficial; it was genuine. You could feel the warmth and care radiating from her as she took the time to listen and guide. She had an innate ability to read the room and know exactly what each situation demanded, whether it was firm leadership or a compassionate ear.

Do you have someone like that in your life? Someone whose charisma is intertwined with their character, making them a constant source of inspiration and guidance? If you do, you'll understand how invaluable such a person is—both as a role model and as a reminder of the kind of teacher and leader we can all strive to become.

Integrating the Four Charisma Types

Type of Charisma	Description	How it Enhances Teaching	Example
Focus Charisma	Deep engagement and attentiveness in interactions, showing genuine interest.	Builds trust and rapport, creating a supportive and engaging learning environment.	A teacher listens intently to a student's concerns, providing thoughtful feedback that makes the student feel valued.
Visionary Charisma	Inspires and motivates by presenting a compelling	Aligns students and colleagues with a shared goal, driving collective progress	A teacher motivates their class by outlining a clear vision of how

	vision for the future.	and enthusiasm.	mastering a subject will benefit their future success.
Kindness Charisma	Demonstrates empathy and compassion, fostering a nurturing atmosphere.	Creates a safe, caring space where students feel valued and supported.	A teacher comforts a stressed student, offering words of encouragement and understanding to boost their confidence.
Authority Charisma	Commands respect and provide a structure for effective leadership.	Ensures that guidance is followed, balancing discipline with expectations for student success.	A teacher sets clear rules in the classroom and holds students accountable, fostering respect and orderly conduct.

Conclusion

As we wrap up this journey together, I hope you've gathered valuable principles, techniques, and strategies that will help you enhance your charisma and leadership in meaningful ways.

Before you close this book, may I ask for a few things?

If this book resonated with you, here's how you can continue to grow and share these insights:

★ **Put what you've learned into action**: Take the concepts you've discovered here and apply them in your everyday life. Share these lessons with your colleagues, and break them down for your students or children in ways they can easily understand. Encourage them to develop their own charisma from a young age. (Remember, today's kids are digitally savvy, socially aware, and absorb new skills quickly.)

★ **Reflect on your charisma regularly**: Take the time to assess your own charisma quotient and be consciously aware of how you're practicing it in different situations. With regular effort, these traits will become second nature. (Just like learning to swim or drive, charisma is a skill that improves with consistent practice.)

★ **Share the gift of charisma**: Don't let this book gather dust on your shelf—pass it on to a colleague or friend. By sharing these insights, you're helping others develop their charisma too. (True charisma isn't just about personal gain; it's about empowering others to achieve greatness.)

So, let's step into our potential, share our light, and make the world a little brighter, one moment at a time.

References

Chapter 1: Stepping into the Charisma Classroom

1. Fond, G., Ducasse, D., Attal, J., Larue, A., Macgregor, A., Brittner, M., & Capdevielle, D. (2012). *Charisma and Leadership in Psychiatry: A Review*. Psychiatry Research, 199(3), 233-238.
2. House, R. J., & Aditya, R. N. (1997). *The Social Scientific Study of Leadership: Quo Vadis?*. Journal of Management, 23(3), 409-473. [Link to Journal]

Chapter 2: Unpacking the Secrets of Charisma

1. "The Charisma Myth" by Olivia Fox Cabane
2. "Captivate: The Science of Succeeding with People" by Vanessa Van Edwards –
3. "Emotional Intelligence" by Daniel Goleman
4. Research by Dr. Ellen Berscheid and Dr. Elaine Walster
5. Study by Daniel Gilbert
6. Riteish Deshmukh's Interview on Netflix India's YouTube Channel
7. TED Talks by Vanessa Van Edwards and Olivia Fox Cabane

Chapter 3: The Charisma Formula

1. The Charisma Myth by Olivia Fox Cabane
2. Captivate: The Science of Succeeding with People by Vanessa Van Edwards
3. Cues: Master the Secret Language of Charismatic Communication by Vanessa Van Edwards

4. Fiske, Susan T., Cuddy, Amy J. C., Glick, Peter, & Xu, Jun (2002). *Journal of Personality and Social Psychology, 82(6), 878-902.*

5. Princeton University Study on Charisma (referenced in Vanessa Van Edwards' book "Cues")

6. TED Talk: "The Power of Body Language" by Amy Cuddy

Chapter 4: The Power of Words

1. "The Charisma Myth" by Olivia Fox Cabane

2. "Captivate: The Science of Succeeding with People" by Vanessa Van Edwards

3. "The Role of Language in Leadership: A Review of the Literature" (Journal of Leadership & Organizational Studies)

4. "The Impact of Verbal Communication on Group Dynamics" (Journal of Applied Psychology)

5. "Verbal Communication and Classroom Management: The Role of Teachers' Language in Effective Teaching" (Teaching and Teacher Education Journal)

6. Harvard Business Review (hbr.org)

7. Psychology Today (psychologytoday.com)

8. American Psychological Association (APA) - apa.org

9. "The Influence of Language on Leadership Effectiveness" (Leadership Quarterly)

10. "The Power of Positive Language in Education" (Educational Psychology Review)

Chapter 5: Speaking Without Words

1. Mehrabian, A. (1971). *Silent Messages: Implicit Communication of Emotions and Attitudes.* Wadsworth Publishing.

2. Cuddy, A. J. C., Wolf, E. B., Glick, P., Crotty, S., Chong, J., & Norton, M. I. (2015). *"Liberating Nonverbal Behavior: The*

Influence of Power Posing on Hormones and Behavior." Psychological Science, 26(12), 1757-1768.

3. Argyle, M., & Dean, J. (1965). *"Eye Contact, Distance, and Affiliation." Sociometry*, 28(4), 289-304.

4. Kendon, A. (1990). *"Conducting Interaction: Patterns of Behavior in Focused Encounters." Cambridge University Press.*

5. Ekman, P. (1972). *"Universal Facial Expressions of Emotion." California Mental Health Research Digest*, 10(2), 151-155.

6. Goldin-Meadow, S. (2003). *"Hearing Gesture: How Our Hands Help Us Think." Harvard University Press.*

7. Kendon, A. (2004). *"Gesture: Visible Action as Utterance." Cambridge University Press.*

8. Matsumoto, D., & Hwang, H. S. (2011). *"Nonverbal Communication: Science and Applications." SAGE Publications.*

9. McNeill, D. (1992). *"Gesture and Thought." University of Chicago Press.*

Chapter 6: The Charismatic Voice

1. Knapp, M. L., & Hall, J. A. (2010). *Nonverbal Communication in Human Interaction* (7th ed.). Wadsworth Publishing.

2. Mehrabian, A. (1971). *Silent Messages: Implicit Communication of Emotions and Attitudes.* Wadsworth Publishing Company.

3. Cleveland, W. (2002). *Speech Communication and the Classroom Teacher*. McGraw-Hill.

4. Apple, W., Streeter, L. A., & Krauss, R. M. (1979). *Effects of Pitch and Speech Rate on Personal Attributions*. Journal of Personality and Social Psychology, 37(5), 715-727.

5. Beebe, S. A., & Beebe, S. J. (2010). *Public Speaking: An Audience-Centered Approach* (8th ed.). Allyn & Bacon.

6. Giles, H., & Oxford, G. (1970). *Towards a Multidimensional Theory of Speech Behavior*. Psychological Bulletin, 74(5), 357-364.

7. McGarrigle, J., & Donaldson, M. (1974). *Speech Rates and Listener Comprehension*. Cognitive Psychology, 6(2), 157-167.

8. Bavelas, J. B., Coates, L., & Johnson, T. (1986). *Listener Responses as a Collaborative Process: The Role of Gaze, Head Nods, and Pauses in Dialogue*. Journal of Personality and Social Psychology, 50(2), 301-308.

9. Fox Tree, J. E. (1999). *Listening in on Monologues and Dialogues*. Discourse Processes, 27(1), 35-53.

10. Zuckerman, M., Hodgins, H. S., & Miyake, K. (2014). *Dramatic Effects of Pauses in Communication*. Psychology Today.

Chapter 7: Charisma in the Classroom: Engaging Students

1. Milojkovic, M., & Zimbardo, P. (1980). *The Psychology of Charisma: Teachers and Leaders in Action*. HarperCollins.

2. Bruner, J. (1996). *The Culture of Education*. Harvard University Press.

3. Kaplan, R. M., & Pascoe, G. C. (1977). *Humor and Its Effect on Learning in Educational Settings*. Journal of Educational Psychology, 69(1), 61-65.

4. Jones, E. E., & Pittman, T. S. (1982). *Toward a General Theory of Strategic Self-Presentation*. In J. Suls (Ed.), *Psychological Perspectives on the Self*, Vol. 1 (pp. 231-261). Lawrence Erlbaum.

5. Keller, J. M. (1987). *Development and Use of the ARCS Model of Motivational Design*. Journal of Instructional Development, 10(3), 2-10.

6. Stipek, D. J. (2002). *Motivation to Learn: Integrating Theory and Practice*. Allyn & Bacon.

7. Giles, H., & Coupland, N. (1991). *Language: Contexts and Consequences*. Open University Press.

8. Warwick, P., & Mercer, N. (2011). *Using Dialogic Teaching to Develop Classroom Interaction and Engagement in Middle Schools*. Journal of Educational Psychology, 103(2), 349-360.

9. Wood, W., & Freeman, L. (2012). *Humor in the Classroom: The Power of Laughter in Learning*. Pedagogical Studies, 17(4), 345-367.

10. Frymier, A. B., & Houser, M. L. (2000). *The Role of Student Engagement in Promoting Effective Learning and Teaching*. Communication Education, 49(4), 297-310.

Chapter 8: Commanding the Meeting Room

1. "The Charisma Myth" by Olivia Fox Cabane

2. "Captivate: The Science of Succeeding with People" by Vanessa Van Edwards

3. Bruner, Jerome. "Actual Minds, Possible Worlds" (Discusses the power of narrative and storytelling in cognition)

4. Heath, Chip, and Heath, Dan. "Made to Stick: Why Some Ideas Survive and Others Die" (On the impact of stories in making ideas memorable)

5. Goleman, D. (1998). "What Makes a Leader?" *Harvard Business Review*. (Leadership skills, emotional intelligence)

6. Riggio, R. E., and Reichard, R. J. (2008). "The Emotional and Social Intelligences of Effective Leadership" *Journal of Managerial Psychology*.

- Bodie, Graham D. (2011). "The Active-Empathic Listening Scale (AELS): Conceptualization and Evidence of Validity within the Interpersonal Domain" *Communication Quarterly*.

- Brownell, Judi. (2012). "Listening: Attitudes, Principles, and Skills" (9th Edition)
- Morgan, N. (2008). "How to Become an Authentic Speaker" *Harvard Business Review.*
- Duarte, N. (2010). "Resonate: Present Visual Stories that Transform Audiences"

Chapter 9: Influencing the Staffroom

1. *The Charisma Myth: How Anyone Can Master the Art and Science of Personal Magnetism* by Olivia Fox Cabane
2. *Captivate: The Science of Succeeding with People* by Vanessa Van Edwards
3. Rogers, C. R., & Farson, R. E. (1957). *Active Listening.* University of Chicago Press.
4. "The Role of Recognition in Enhancing Employee Motivation" by James K. Harter, published in *Gallup Business Journal.*
5. "Emotional Intelligence and Its Impact on Employee Performance" by Daniel Goleman, published in *Harvard Business Review.*
6. "Diversity and Inclusion: The Power of Recognizing Differences" by David Rock, published in *Forbes.*
7. "The Benefits of Celebrating Diversity in the Workplace" by Michael C. Hyter, published in *Forbes.*

Chapter 10: Mastering in Parent-Teacher Meetings

1. "The Charisma Myth: How Anyone Can Master the Art and Science of Personal Magnetism" by Olivia Fox Cabane
2. "The Importance of Assertiveness in Education" – Educational Research Review

3. "Parent-Teacher Communication: Strategies for Effective Collaboration" – Journal of Educational Psychology

4. "Handling Difficult Conversations: Techniques for Educators" – Teaching and Teacher Education Journal

5. Edutopia: "Effective Parent-Teacher Conferences: Tips and Strategies"

6. MindTools: "Assertiveness Techniques: How to Be Assertive at Work"

7. Harvard Business Review: "How to Give Feedback that Actually Works"

8. American Psychological Association (APA): "Managing Difficult Conversations in School Settings"

9. The National Education Association (NEA): "Best Practices for Parent-Teacher Conferences"

10. The Center for Responsive Schools: "Communicating with Parents: Building Strong Partnerships"

Chapter 11: Charisma With Integrity

1. Cabane, Olivia Fox. *The Charisma Myth: How Anyone Can Master the Art and Science of Personal Magnetism..*

2. Van Edwards, Vanessa. *Captivate: The Science of Succeeding with People.*

3. Van Edwards, Vanessa. *The Charisma Cues: How to Master the Science of Personal Magnetism.*

4. Northouse, Peter G. *Leadership: Theory and Practice.* Sage Publications, 2018.

5. Gardner, Howard. *Leading Minds: An Anatomy of Leadership.* Basic Books, 1995.

6. Judge, Timothy A., and Ronald F. Piccolo. "The Forgotten Ones? The Validity of Consideration and Initiating Structure in

Leadership Research." *Journal of Applied Psychology*, vol. 92, no. 1, 2007, pp. 36–47.

7. Cuddy, Amy J. C., and Peter Glick. "The Effects of Warmth and Competence on Interpersonal Judgments." *Social Psychological and Personality Science*, vol. 2, no. 3, 2011, pp. 266–274.

8. Avolio, Bruce J., and William L. Gardner. "Authentic Leadership Development: Getting to the Root of Positive Forms of Leadership." *The Leadership Quarterly*, vol. 16, no. 3, 2005, pp. 315–338.

Acknowledgments

I am immensely grateful to so many people who made this book possible!

First and foremost, thank you for taking the time to read it. I extend my heartfelt appreciation to all the teachers who have crossed paths with me over the past decade. Your shared experiences have shaped my understanding and enriched my perspective on teaching. I know how challenging this journey can be, and I get it! This book is written to help you navigate the everyday challenges we teachers face. If even one teacher, student, or colleague is positively influenced by the ideas in this book, the effort has been worth it.

A huge thank you to the incredible Active Kids team for sharing their virtual classroom insights, which deepened my understanding of modern education.

Thank you to my entire family, especially my parents, Khurshid Pathan and Fayaz Pathan, for their unwavering support. To my friends and support system—thank you for the countless pep talks, encouragement, and love.

Mansoor Sheikh, you are the best business and life partner I could have ever asked for. Your belief in me has been my greatest strength.

And to the light of my life, my daughter Arshiya Sheikh, thank you for being my constant source of inspiration and joy.

Verses Kindler Publication

Reach us through our website -
https://www.verseskindlerpublication.com/
For more information visit our Instagram or Facebook page.

www.ingramcontent.com/pod-product-compliance
Lightning Source LLC
Chambersburg PA
CBHW041200150726
48006CB00016B/2051